FINDING THE WAY

USA TODAY Bestselling Author

Ruth Hartzler

HARLEQUIN

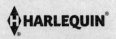

ISBN-13: 978-1-335-49910-3

Finding the Way

First published in 2018 by Ruth Hartzler.
This edition published in 2020.

This edition published by arrangement with Harlequin Books S.A.

For questions and comments about the quality of this book, please contact us at CustomerService@Harlequin.com.

Harlequin Enterprises ULC
22 Adelaide St. West, 40th Floor
Toronto, Ontario M5H 4E3, Canada
www.Harlequin.com

Printed in U.S.A.

Recycling programs for this product may not exist in your area.

"You are here to try to take me back home."

Benjamin hesitated, and Sarah hoped he would deny it. She held her breath, but his answer crashed her hopes. "That's part of it," he said, avoiding her eyes.

"I know he's sent you to bring me back," she snapped. "I won't go back."

"Your father," Benjamin began, but Sarah cut him short.

"He's *not* my father," she spat.

For the second time in as many minutes, Benjamin's mouth opened in surprise. "Sarah, isn't that a bit harsh?" he began. "I do realize he is a stern *mann*, but he is your *vadder* after all."

So he doesn't know, Sarah thought.

A gust of wind chose that moment to blow off Sarah's prayer *kapp*. She clutched at it wildly and nearly overbalanced into the pond. Benjamin seized her and pulled her back to safety, but that caused her to be pulled hard against his muscular chest.

Benjamin's strong arms around her waist sent butterflies through Sarah's stomach. *Maybe there is hope after all*, she thought.

USA TODAY bestselling author **Ruth Hartzler** was a college professor of biblical history and ancient languages. Now she writes faith-based romances, cozy mysteries and archaeological thrillers. She is best known for her Amish romances, which were inspired by her Anabaptist upbringing. When Ruth is not writing, she spends her time walking her dog and baking cakes for her adult children, all of whom have food allergies. Ruth also enjoys correcting grammar on shop signs when nobody is looking.

FINDING THE WAY

Chapter One

Sarah Beachy bent through the reeds, staring at her reflection in the pond near the Millers' *haus*. Not that the pond showed an accurate depiction of her face, for the wafting breeze caused gentle ripples to form on the water's surface. Five happy ducklings splashed around, sending a water strider spider scuttling and distorting Sarah's reflection even further. The breeze grew in momentum, whipping her long, blonde hair out from under her prayer *kapp* and swirling it around her face.

Sarah sat back and smiled. She had found peace in Lancaster, with its rolling hills and green pastures, far away from her recent times of turmoil and strife. There were serious questions as yet unanswered, but for today, she was happy to spend time alone and enjoy the beauty of *Gott's* creation.

Sarah watched some bluebirds on a far branch, idly thinking she was glad that her somewhat overweight ginger cat, Tom, was not interested in catching birds.

He's too lazy to catch anything, she thought with a smile. The bluebirds were the same colors as the Spinning Star quilt Sarah was currently working on for Mrs. Hostetler's store. The quilt, like the bluebirds, featured vivid blue contrasting with the rich, earthy tones of brown. *There are no better colors than the ones that Gott has designed*, she thought.

The small flock of bluebirds suddenly took to the skies, startling her. Sarah looked up to see what had put them to flight, wondering if it could be a fox, or even a horse grazing in the field. She saw a figure advancing in the distance. It was not a fox, or a horse, but a *mann*, but not just any *mann*. Even from a distance, Sarah could see this *mann* was Benjamin Shetler.

Sarah hurried to repin her hair under the *kapp*. The wind was blowing wildly now, in keeping with her emotions. She stood and faced Benjamin's approach.

As he came toward her, Sarah tried to tear her eyes away from him. Benjamin always made her heart thump wildly. Her gaze traveled over his arms bronzed from a lifetime of farm work, his broad shoulders, and mess of sandy colored hair poking out in all directions from under his straw hat. Benjamin had a commanding presence, even out here in the fields.

Benjamin was beautiful, perhaps not so much on the outside for, despite his youth, he had a rugged look imparted by years of working in the sun, but there was an inner beauty that radiated from him. He was kind, gentle, and caring, and was truly a man of *Gott*.

Yet Sarah had to steel herself to deny the heart-wrenching attraction she felt for Benjamin, for she could not trust him. He had proven that, even though Sarah knew that he thought he was doing the right thing. Even more so, she had known him since they were children, but he had never asked her on a buggy ride. As Benjamin clearly did not want to court her, why hadn't *Gott* taken away her feelings for him? Goodness knows she had asked Him to many a time. It hurt too much.

Sarah's mouth ran dry and she licked her lips nervously. She knew why Benjamin was seeking her out, and she was far from pleased. She had known this day would come.

"I know why you're here." Sarah was dismayed her voice sounded so harsh and accusatory, but she had no idea how to handle this situation.

Benjamin appeared to be taken aback. "I'm not sure you do," he said slowly.

Sarah looked away from his big brown eyes and stared at the trees on the other side of the pond. "You are here to try to take me back home." Her slow, measured tone gave no hint of the strong emotions coursing through her.

Benjamin hesitated, and Sarah hoped he would deny it. She held her breath, but his answer crashed her hopes. "That's part of it," he said, avoiding her eyes.

"I know he's sent you to bring me back," she snapped. "I won't go back."

"Your father," Benjamin began, but Sarah cut him short.

"He's *not* my father," she spat.

For the second time in as many minutes, Benjamin's mouth opened in surprise. "Sarah, isn't that a bit harsh?" he began. "I do realize he is a stern *mann*, but he is your *vadder* after all."

So he doesn't know, Sarah thought.

A gust of wind chose that moment to blow off Sarah's prayer *kapp*. She clutched at it wildly and nearly overbalanced into the pond. Benjamin seized her and pulled her back to safety, but that caused her to be pulled hard against his muscular chest.

Benjamin's strong arms around her waist sent butterflies through Sarah's stomach. Her heart beat so loudly she was afraid Benjamin would hear it. Yet she made no attempt to leave the safety of his arms, and he held her to him far longer than was necessary. *Maybe there is hope after all*, she thought.

After what seemed an age, Sarah detached herself. She turned her back to Benjamin while she pinned her prayer *kapp*, more carefully this time.

The long silence hung heavy and uneasy between them. The tension grew thick. Finally, Sarah could stand it no longer. "He's *not* my *vadder*," she repeated, and before Benjamin could protest again, she added, "He is not my biological father."

Benjamin did not speak, so Sarah turned around to look at him. *He looks truly surprised*, she thought, *so he mustn't have known*.

"Shall we walk, and you can tell me all about it?"

Sarah nodded, thankful for Benjamin's kind and understanding manner, and walked quietly beside him along the dirt road that ran by the pond in the general direction of the B&B. The clip clop of a horse's hooves bore down behind them fast, so they both waited to greet the driver.

The big, black horse was pulled to an abrupt stop beside them, and Jessie Yoder looked down at them. "You two look cozy," she said, her tone dripping with sarcasm. The horse arched his neck and pawed the ground, eager to be on his way.

"*Hiya,* Jessie," Sarah said in her most polite voice.

"Sorry, no time for idle chit-chat! I'm late for my first day at work." Jessie slapped the horse hard with the reins and he took off fast toward the B&B.

"Not the most polite girl I've ever met," Benjamin said, although Sarah detected amusement in his voice. "Mrs. Flickinger says she's sure Jessie will work just as hard at the B&B as Rebecca does. Still, Jessie doesn't appear to be your typical Amish *maidel.*"

Sarah shook her head. "*Nee.* She gave Esther a hard time. In fact, she kept Esther and Jacob apart for a while."

"Oh well, they're together now, that's all that counts."

"*Jah.*" Sarah was embarrassed for gossiping and was worried that Benjamin would think less of her. Yet what did Benjamin actually think of her at all? She had no idea.

Benjamin stopped to pick a blue violet growing

alongside other wildflowers by the dirt road, and handed it to Sarah.

She took it, looking up at Benjamin, wondering what this gesture meant and indeed, if it meant anything at all.

"You don't have to tell me if you don't want to," Benjamin said, breaking the moment.

"*Nee*, it's okay. As you know, *Mamm* died." Benjamin nodded and Sarah continued. "And after the funeral, my *daed*"—she hesitated using the word—"told me that *Mamm* had been married before."

Benjamin gasped and came to a stop, but Sarah kept walking. "He told me that my real father had died when I was three months old, and *Mamm* had remarried that same year. Well, she married him, of course, my *daed*, I mean." Sarah now came to a stop, and waved her hands in agitation. "This is confusing to try to explain."

"*Nee*, I understand," Benjamin said. "Your *daed* and your *mudder* had you, and then your *daed* passed away, and your *mudder* remarried Samuel Beachy, the *mann* who you always thought was your *daed*."

Sarah nodded and twirled the pretty blue flower around between her fingers. "It was such a shock to me, *Mamm* dying, and then finding out that he was not my biological father. Such a shock," she repeated.

Benjamin shrugged. "Is that why you left, so suddenly?"

Sarah stomped her foot. "*Jah*! They both lied to me all these years. Why wouldn't they tell me the truth? I don't even know the name of my real *vadder*."

Chapter Two

Jessie Yoder arrived at the Flickingers' B&B with some trepidation, nodding to Rebecca as she walked up the stairs. Rebecca obviously wasn't surprised to see her, so clearly Mrs. Flickinger had forewarned her.

Jessie was concerned about working there. She was not afraid of hard work—after all, she was Amish— but she didn't much like meeting with people, much less speaking with them. Jessie would be happy if she never spoke to another person again. She found people rather irritating.

And so, when Mrs. Flickinger met her with a wide smile, it was all Jessie could do to return the smile. "Come into the kitchen and share a nice cup of garden tea with me," Mrs. Flickinger said.

Jessie's spirits sank. She was hoping she could get straight to work, but it looked as though there was going to be some sort of interview process. The bishop had given her to understand the job was hers.

Maybe it was, and Mrs. Flickinger just wanted to get acquainted. She winced as she thought of all the small talk that was surely to come.

Mrs. Flickinger indicated Jessie should sit down, and she fussed around preparing the tea, which she duly placed in front of Jessie, along with a plate of Shoo-fly pie. "The bishop tells me you're an ideal person to help here," Mrs. Flickinger said.

Jessie nodded slowly. She had no idea why the bishop had said such a thing, but she wasn't about to ask. Mrs. Flickinger pushed on. "With Rebecca marrying Elijah Hostetler soon enough, there will be time for the two of you to work together and learn the ropes."

Jessie nodded once more. She didn't mind Rebecca too much. After all, Rebecca didn't really get on her nerves as she didn't speak often. Jessie felt she could work quite amicably with Rebecca.

"I must warn you about my son, Eli. He likes to call himself Nash. Please don't let him push you around. He can be rather, err, unpleasant at times."

"I won't let him push me around," Jessie said truthfully. *I'd like to see him try*, she added silently. She had heard about Nash Grayson and had seen him once or twice. She found him fascinating, but she wasn't going to take any of his nonsense. She had heard he was quite the troublemaker. Jessie smiled to herself.

"There is just the general cleaning to do," Mrs. Flickinger continued. "It's just like a typical Amish home, only bigger. And, of course, the bishop has allowed us to have electricity here because of the business. Rebecca can show you how to work the electric vacuum and the other electrical items. Try to keep out of the way of the guests, and if they ask you any questions, then simply refer them to me."

"That won't be a problem," Jessie said. She had no desire to speak with any of the guests, although she did find *Englischers* fascinating.

"So like I said, it's cleaning. You would be used to all of it and it won't take you long to get used to the electrical appliances. If the phone rings, I'll get it, or Rebecca can get it. You can move on to that later on, but for now just get used to the place and the cleaning and the electrical appliances. I'll call for Rebecca now to show you around."

Mrs. Flickinger slipped out the door to summon Rebecca. Jessie took advantage of her absence to study the kitchen. It did indeed look just like any other Amish kitchen, only immeasurably bigger. Jessie had heard this was an old Mennonite building that had been turned into a B&B so that made sense. However, the huge refrigerator was obviously electric and there was an electric oven and cooktop. The preparation areas were stainless steel. Jessie figured it had been renovated at some point to make it commercial. She had not used an electric vacuum before, but how hard could it be? She figured there was no electric way to wash floors, so she would be used to that. She was still lost in her thoughts when Mrs. Flickinger returned with Rebecca.

"*Hiya*, Jessie," Rebecca said.

"*Hiya*, Rebecca," Jessie responded.

"Now Rebecca will show you around and show you the ropes," Mrs. Flickinger said in a cheery voice.

"I'll show you the house and the unoccupied bedrooms first," Rebecca said as the two of them walked out the door. Jessie silently counseled herself to be nice. She would find it difficult working there if she said anything snarky to Rebecca, so she held her peace.

"There is Wi-Fi here, you know, internet, for the guests," Rebecca explained. "There's a card with a password in their rooms, but sometimes the guests will ask for it. You just have to tell them the card is in the room on the nightstand."

"Mrs. Flickinger told me not to speak with any of the guests," Jessie said.

Rebecca simply shrugged one shoulder. "This is the dining room. I suppose that's obvious." She broke off with a laugh. "Come on, I'll show you the rest of the rooms."

Jessie traipsed after Rebecca. She was already bored and couldn't wait to start working. She didn't know why she had to be shown the rooms. After all, this tour was exceedingly boring. It was not as if there was anything exciting to see.

And that was when Rebecca opened the door to the west sitting room. Jessie gasped. Rebecca laughed. "Nash decorated this room himself. He sold the Flickingers' buggy horse to the widow Ramseyer to raise the money for that huge television and the rest of it. The Flickingers are going to repaint it, but they haven't had a chance as the guests are quite fond of this room."

"Why would they be fond of this room?" Jessie asked.

"The television, I expect," Rebecca said.

Jessie nodded slowly. "Of course. Interesting choice of color."

Rebecca chuckled. "Nash said it was important that a room stands out and is not forgettable."

"This room sure isn't forgettable," Jessie said, staring at the fluorescent green furniture.

"Nash said it glows in the dark," Rebecca told her.

Nash sounded more and more interesting to Jessie. She couldn't wait to meet him. "And Nash lives here at the B&B?"

"Yes, he lives permanently in one of the guest rooms here," Rebecca said with a sigh. "I must warn you about him. He expects me to clean up after him and he expects his mother to clean up after him too."

Jessie pulled a face. "He sounds like a spoiled brat," she said.

Rebecca simply bit her lip and shrugged one shoulder again.

This Nash guy must be really bad because Rebecca didn't jump to his defense like the do-gooder that she is, Jessie thought. Jessie was increasingly intrigued by him.

"Come on, I'll show you the vacant bedrooms."

"Did Nash decorate any of those?" Jessie asked Rebecca.

Rebecca shook her head and laughed. "*Nee.*"

Jessie was disappointed. She was more disappointed when she was shown one bedroom after another. They were all the same typical Amish rooms. They were sparse with barely any furniture although they did have colorful Amish quilts on the beds. They had large closets rather than pegs on the wall on which to hang clothes.

Jessie crossed the room and looked out the window. It was certainly a beautiful view and she could understand why people came here.

Rebecca turned to her. "Well, my duties, I mean our duties, are to clean everything when the guests leave. There is a lot of laundry to do too." She tapped herself on the head. "Oh, that reminds me! We have an electric washing machine and an electric clothes dryer."

Jessie's spirits lifted. "You do?" she said, intrigued. She had never seen an electric washing machine or an electric clothes dryer before. If there was one thing Jessie hated doing, it was laundry. "I expect that makes doing the laundry go quite fast."

Rebecca nodded with a smile. "It sure does."

"Then what's left to do?"

Rebecca chuckled. "Plenty! It takes a while to clean the guest rooms as most of the guests leave things in a mess. When guests leave, we replace the linen and wash the old linen and dry it, and we have to vacuum the floors and wash the floors, and there are lots of windows to wash. I've not been able to keep up with it by myself lately, and Mrs. Flickinger has been helping me, but her arthritis has been playing up more and more. I expect when I leave, she will need to hire someone else to help."

"So you won't still work here when you marry Elijah?"

Rebecca shook her head. "Elijah is going to buy a farm of his own and I'll be helping him with it. There will be no time to help here."

Jessie bit her lip, processing the information.

"I was about to vacuum the west sitting room. The guests usually start watching the television early in the day, so I like to get it done fairly quickly."

"They watch television early in the day?" Jessie repeated in surprise. "Don't they go out and do tourist things?"

"Sometimes," Rebecca said, "but sometimes they like to start their day with watching TV and coffee."

Jessie found that puzzling, but then again she found *Englischers* puzzling at the best of times. Soon she found herself back in the west sitting room standing under a black ceiling and surrounded by vivid purple walls.

"Now this is how it works," Rebecca said. "You just put this into the outlet like so." Jessie watched what Rebecca did. "Now see this button here. You just press it." Rebecca pressed the button and Jessie took an involuntary step backward as the machine whirred to life. It was so loud that Jessie fought the urge to put her fingers in her ears. "It's loud," she said somewhat unnecessarily.

Rebecca chuckled. "You'll get used to it. Now you just do this." Rebecca showed her what to do. "And there you go." She turned off the machine. "Now see here—you can flick the switch here to the carpet setting."

"Why is that?" Jessie asked, intrigued.

"It's just that it vacuums at different suction rates for carpet and for hardwood floors," Rebecca explained. "Here, have a go."

Jessie gleefully seized the machine from Rebecca. She switched it on and it whirred into action once more. She found using it quite a bit of fun. "It's sure easier than sweeping," she said over the noise of the machine.

Rebecca walked over and flipped off the vacuum. "It sure is much better than sweeping!" she said. "Just be careful when you're around any curtains because it will suck those up too. Will you be all right doing this room by yourself?"

"Sure," Jessie said. She far preferred to be working by herself, without the nosy Rebecca looking over her shoulder.

"When you've finished here," Rebecca continued, "just vacuum all the other downstairs rooms. I'll make a start on the laundry and then come and fetch you in a while and show you how to work the washing machine and dryer."

"Sure," Jessie said again.

As soon as Rebecca was out of sight, Jessie hurried over to the nearest curtain. She turned on the machine and stuck the end of the vacuum against the curtain to see what would happen. Sure enough, it sucked up the curtain quickly.

Jessie stood back, horrified. She had no idea it would do something like that. She had thought Rebecca was exaggerating. It took her a moment to realize she could stop it by turning off the machine. She did so and then pulled the curtain out.

Jessie found some dust in the corner of the room. "That do-gooder Rebecca should have seen to that yesterday," she said aloud. "It's obviously been there a while." She couldn't figure out how to get it out, so did the best she could. After a while, she realized she could take off the end of the vacuum, but she wasn't sure how to do so. She shrugged and went back to vacuuming the rest of the room. She had trouble at first remembering how to flip the switch to carpet when she had to vacuum the bright orange shag rug.

Just then, a tall, thin, tattooed young man entered the room. Jessie realized at once he was Nash Grayson. He walked over to one of the couches and threw himself on it and then picked up a remote and turned on the TV. "Don't mind me," he said to Jessie.

"I won't," Jessie said over her vacuuming. Out of the corner of her eye, she noticed Nash staring at her. When he had come in, she had left the rug and gone back to vacuuming the rest of the room, but now she had to finish the rug and that would be the room done. Nash's feet were on the carpet so she said, "Move your feet. Get out of my way."

He did not move his feet, but looked up at her. "What's the magic word?" he said.

"Magic word?" she repeated, puzzled.

He sighed dramatically. "Please," he said.

Jessie simply frowned at him. "I've told you to move your feet," she said.

Nash looked surprised. "I will if you say 'please,'" he said.

So that's the way it's going to be, Jessie thought. "Suit yourself," she said and rammed the end of the vacuum into Nash's feet.

"Ouch!" He at once lifted his feet into the air. Jessie vacuumed under his feet. He held them in the air until she had finished.

"That hurt," he said.

"Not my problem," Jessie said and continued vacuuming.

"I thought all Amish girls were nice and sweet," he said.

"That's not my problem," Jessie said again. "Anyway, I'm out of here." She pulled the vacuum out of the wall and then hurried out of the room.

Chapter Three

Nash Grayson, or Elijah Flickinger as his parents still called him given it was his birth name, was fascinated by the person of Jessie Yoder. At first he thought she was a humble Amish girl, but that idea was rudely squashed when she first opened her mouth and ordered him in no uncertain terms to get out of the way when she was vacuuming.

Most afternoons, Nash made his way down to the ruins of an old stone cottage, which sat on the slope below the B&B. He liked to sit and ponder his next money-making scheme. He still owed a considerable sum to bookmakers from gambling on racehorses, and his ungrateful, selfish parents still refused to pay his gambling debts. He had no idea why.

Every day, Nash smelled the lingering smell of smoke, and occasionally found cigarette butts. At first he thought it was the *Englischer* guests, but there had not been any *Englischer* guests for two days and he had found a fresh cigarette butt only that day. He very much doubted it was the do-gooder Benjamin Shetler, so the one suspect who remained was Jessie Yoder.

Nash decided to catch Jessie in the act the following day, and all he had to do was change his routine and get up early. And so, that lovely spring morning, he hid behind the stone walls and waited for the cigarette smoker to come.

He did not have to wait long. Nash's stomach tensed with excitement as he heard stones crunch underneath boots. He waited until the sound stopped and then leaped out to confront the cigarette smoker.

"Gotcha!" he yelled, waving his arms in the air. "Jessie Yoder, just as I thought!"

Jessie looked startled momentarily, but then took the cigarette from her lips and blew a long stream of smoke in his direction. "What are you going to do about it?" she said slowly.

Nash was shocked. He expected her to look guilty or at least worried, but she did not, and what's more, her tone was bordering on rude. He had to admire the way she brazened it out. "I'll tell someone," he said.

Jessie laughed. "Who are they going to believe, you, or me?" She waved her hand up and down in his direction, gesturing to his clothes and tattoos.

Nash had not expected that reaction. "Well, um, smoking is the wrong thing to do."

Jessie took another drag. "What's it to you?" she said rudely. "It's none of your business."

Nash was quite put out. He had been expecting the culprit would be guilty when caught. For the first time in his life, he was speechless.

Jessie had not finished with him. "You're an *Englischer* now, right?"

Nash nodded, wondering where she was going with this.

"So you have mirrors, right?"

Nash nodded again.

"Go have a look in the mirror. If you don't see the bishop looking back at you, that means you're not the bishop. So if you're not the bishop, and you're not my *vadder*, you can't tell me what to do. Mind your own business." With that, Jessie flicked her cigarette butt at his feet, and then walked off.

Nash was crestfallen. He had been bested by a girl, and an Amish girl at that. *She's attractive for an Amish girl though*, he thought.

After a time of contemplation over how everyone was mean to him for no good reason, Nash made his way back to the B&B for some coffee and whoopie pies. Getting up so early that morning had made him hungry. If he sneaked into the kitchen, he should be able to score some food, if that greedy Benjamin Shetler hadn't eaten it all. Jessie was now pinning washing on the line, so he wouldn't run into her again.

Nash crept along the corridor, inhaling the scent of freshly brewed *kaffi*, but the sound of his parents whispering in the kitchen pulled him up in his tracks. He tiptoed to the closed door and put his ear against it.

"It was the bishop's wife, Fannie Graber, who let it slip," his *mudder* said. "It made me wonder if Sarah Beachy is, in fact, the adopted *dochder* of Samuel

Beachy, who left our community to marry a widow with a *boppli*."

"That would be a bit of a coincidence though," his *daed* said, "for Sarah Beachy to meet Martha Miller in prison of all places, and then even end up staying with the Millers."

"Perhaps it was *Gott's* plan," his *mudder* said. "Not a coincidence at all."

Nash was unable to hear anything else as his parents lowered their voices even more, so he decided on the bold approach. He opened the door and marched straight in. "No need to stop talking when I come in," he said, noting that his parents exchanged guilty looks. "What were you talking about?"

"Nothing," they both said, and both left the room in a hurry.

Nash shrugged. *Thank goodness they've gone*, he thought. *I won't get into trouble for eating all the food*. He decided to make coffee and eat some sandwiches. *If only I were in the city, I could go to a café and get a proper coffee, not this strong, bitter stuff. Still, it's free*, he thought, spooning several spoons of sugar into his mug. His stoneware coffee mug was white, with a black horse and buggy and a black windmill. "How quaint," he said aloud, with as much sarcasm as he could muster. "I've got to get out of this dump of a place as soon as I can."

Yet, a small, niggling thought ate away at Nash. *If I leave here, I'll be leaving Jessie*. Nash shook his head to try to dismiss the thought from his mind.

After Nash ate all the sandwiches in the refrigerator plus a copious amount of soft pretzels with homemade mustard, he poured himself some more coffee and took it to his room. He sat on the edge of his bed, pulled out his cell phone, and looked at it. *I must get to the bottom of this*, he thought. *What has Sarah Beachy got to do with the Millers?*

Nash could not remember anyone named Samuel Beachy from his community, but if Samuel Beachy had left when Sarah was a *boppli*, then Nash would have been a *boppli* too.

Nash stroked his chin. One of his old friends was still on *rumspringa*. He would call him and ask him to find out everything about Samuel Beachy. Nash was sure there would be some way he could use this to his advantage. If nothing else, it would lift the boredom that had so rapidly descended upon his life, being stuck living with his parents in the boring countryside, surrounded by boring Amish folk.

Chapter Four

Sarah sat awkwardly at the large wooden table in the bishop's wife's kitchen. She was worried on two counts, and both with good reason. Fannie Graber, the bishop's wife, had invited the *youngie* to lunch, and Fannie was known for her strange food choices. This was also the first time Sarah would see Benjamin again after that day by the pond, when she had told him that her real *vadder* had died when she was a *boppli* and, more to the point, when she had fallen and he had caught her in his arms.

Fannie's ample frame bustled over to the table. "Here, have a little something to eat while we wait for the others to arrive," she said, setting plates of what looked like raisin bars in front of Sarah and the other young people.

Sarah was used to Fannie's food, so asked, "What is in them?"

"Why they are raisin and raw liver bars, dear,"

Fannie said, as if she were stating the obvious. "Very good for you, high in iron. Eat up."

To Sarah's relief, the door opened and Benjamin, Nash, and Jessie all arrived at once.

Sarah stared in puzzlement at Nash. After all, he was an *Englischer* now, and not one of the community's *youngie*, but then, Fannie Graber was a kindly soul and probably thought Nash was simply on *rumspringa*. And he might still be, for all she knew, Sarah reminded herself. Sarah noted Nash had removed his piercings, and had rolled down his sleeves to cover his tattoos, despite the day being warm.

As they took their places at the table, Sarah wondered about the pungent perfume wafting from Jessie. Surely she hadn't taken to wearing perfume, and if so, why such a distasteful one? Perhaps Jessie had brushed up against an English guest's car at the B&B, as the scent had somewhat of a stale, mechanical smell mixed with peppermint. It took Sarah a while to realize the odor was cigarette smoke.

Sarah looked up from her musings over Jessie to see Benjamin staring at her. He looked away at once.

Fannie was clearly delighted that all her guests were there, and set many plates of sandwiches on the table. All her guests looked aghast, and opened the sandwiches to look inside them. "What's in your delicious sandwiches today, Mrs. Graber?" Jessie asked with no obvious trace of sarcasm.

"Those ones are plain sugar and pickle sandwiches; those ones are chocolate spread and blue cheese; those ones are anchovy and marmite. Now excuse me a moment; I'll just fetch the pea and ham soup."

Everyone looked at each other, and then all reached for the sugar and pickle sandwiches and put them on their plates. When Fannie returned with a large soup tureen, Jessie asked, "What's in the soup?"

"Why I told you, pea and ham, dear. It *is* called pea and ham soup after all."

Sarah tentatively ladled some soup into her bowl and tasted it gingerly. Much to her surprise, it actually tasted like pea and ham soup. She let out a sigh of relief, but then saw funny little things floating inside the soup. She fished one out and looked at it. It looked like a cashew nut. "Is this a cashew nut, Mrs. Graber?"

Mrs. Graber looked at Sarah as if she were somewhat silly. "Yes, of course. I already told you twice only moments ago that it was pea and ham soup."

Oh well, it could be worse, Sarah thought, as she tucked into the pea and ham—and cashew nut—soup.

Sarah had hoped to speak to Benjamin, but Jessie Yoder was hogging the conversation, flirting with Benjamin and Nash, the only two *menner* her age at the table. Until now, Sarah had never considered that Benjamin would be interested in Jessie, but here he was, laughing at her jokes and generally getting on well with her. *Jessie works at the B&B, and Benjamin is a guest there*, Sarah thought with dismay, suddenly assaulted by uncomfortable pangs of jealousy.

Sarah shook her head to try to clear it. *Benjamin isn't interested in me*, she thought, *or he would have asked me on a buggy ride ages ago, before I left my community and came here. He's only here to try to force me to go back.* Once more, she sent up a silent prayer to *Gott* to ask Him to take away her feelings for Benjamin.

Mrs. Graber addressed Sarah. "I hear your cousin is coming to stay with the Millers."

Sarah shook her head. "*Nee*, she isn't my cousin, she's my friend, but *jah*, she is coming to stay with me at the Millers' *haus* for a few weeks."

Fannie Graber reached across and patted Sarah's hand. "And that will be good company for you. What with Mary and David courting and Rebecca and Elijah courting, you must feel all alone."

Sarah wished Mrs. Graber hadn't quite put it like that, and she did not miss Nash's smirk in her direction.

Mrs. Graber pushed on. "So, does your friend have a *mann* of her own? And what is her name?"

Sarah figured that Fannie Graber already knew her friend's name as she knew much about everything in these parts. "Beth," she said. "We've been friends for many years."

"But she is not from your community," Fannie prompted her.

Aha, so she does know all about her, Sarah thought. Aloud she said, "*Nee*, we grew up together, but then her father died and her mother married a man from another community and they moved there. We write each other letters all the time and occasionally visit each other and stay for some time."

"And does she have a young man of her own?" Mrs. Graber prompted her.

"*Nee*." Sarah shifted awkwardly in her seat.

Mrs. Graber chuckled. "Well, I'm sure Rachel Miller will soon find a man for her." She looked at both Benjamin and Nash.

Sarah wondered who Mrs. Graber had in mind. Surely not Nash? He was hardly suitable for an Amish girl, so that only left Benjamin. A sharp pang of jealousy hit her like a knife going into her chest. She knew it was irrational, because Beth knew how she felt about Benjamin. What's more, Beth was not interested in Benjamin for herself, but Sarah supposed that jealousy was irrational at the best of times.

She looked up to see Nash smirking at her once more. "Who do you think Mrs. Miller will choose for Beth?" he asked Mrs. Graber.

"Oh, I've never been successful at matchmaking, not like Rachel Miller," Mrs. Graber said with a dismissive wave of her hand. "There are several eligible young *menner* in the community. Mrs. Miller successfully found matches for all her daughters as well as for Mary. She will find a suitable match for Beth in no time. You wait and see. I'm surprised she hasn't found someone for you yet, Sarah." She wagged her finger at Sarah.

Sarah wished that the ground would open up and swallow her on the spot. She hadn't missed the look that Benjamin shot her. But what did it mean? How did Benjamin feel about her? She had never been able to figure that out and probably never would.

"Now you look like a horse with that long face," Mrs. Graber said. "I know, chocolate will make you feel better. Don't be sad because you're all alone at your age, Sarah. Rachel has always been successful in her matchmaking endeavors."

With that, she left the room with a chuckle. Sarah thought she should speak to break the awkward silence that had descended upon the table. "So, do you like working at the B&B?" She addressed the question to Jessie.

Jessie looked up at her, narrowed her eyes, and offered a curt, "*Jah*."

"I think Jessie likes the company," Nash said with a pointed look at Benjamin.

To Sarah's surprise, Jessie elbowed Nash hard in the ribs. He doubled over and let out a yell. "What was that for?" he said.

"Sometimes you go too far, Nash," Jessie spat.

Sarah wondered what all that was about, but her attention was soon diverted by Fannie Graber's return. She placed a plate of what looked like regular chocolate whoopie pies on the table. In fact, her next words confirmed it. "Chocolate whoopie pies," she said. "Eat up, Sarah. There's nothing like chocolate to mend a broken heart."

"But, but I don't have a broken heart," Sarah sputtered. That wasn't quite the truth, but she had no idea what Mrs. Graber meant.

"What's in them, Mrs. Graber?" Jessie asked. She picked one up and turned it over and over in her hands.

"Why, just the usual ingredients," Mrs. Graber said with surprise. "They're just regular old whoopie pies. You know, flour, buttermilk, cocoa powder, vanilla, marshmallow cream, butter, baking soda, anchovies and finely diced sardine heads, and red pepper."

Jessie at once put the whoopie pie on Nash's plate and he ate it in one gulp.

Sarah leaned forward and rubbed her temples with both hands. *Could this be any worse?* she thought. *I just want to go home and lock myself in my room. I can't wait until Beth gets here.*

Although she had not said the words aloud, Nash looked up from eating his second whoopie pie. "So tell me about your friend, Beth," he said. "Is she good-looking?"

Mrs. Graber gasped. "Nash, you should know better than to ask such a question," she scolded him, albeit in kindly tones. "It's not what's on the outside of a person that counts. God looks at the outside and not the inside."

"But I'm not God," Nash said, "and I always look at the outside of a person." He clutched his stomach and laughed at his own joke. The fact that no one laughed with him did not seem to perturb him in the slightest.

"Well, I'm sure Sarah's friend won't date an *Englischer*," Mrs. Graber pointed out.

Nash appeared affronted. "I wasn't asking for myself."

Mrs. Graber scratched her head. "Then who were

you asking for? Are you doing a spot of matchmaking yourself, Nash?" She chuckled.

Nash flushed beet red. *He's up to something*, Sarah thought, *but what?* She noticed that Jessie was visibly annoyed. The two of them seemed good friends, so Sarah wondered if they could possibly be plotting something together. She let out a long sigh. *I can't wait until Beth gets here*, she thought once more.

Nash helped himself to some more Applesauce Cake Surprise. He had no idea what the surprise was, and he didn't care, even if it did taste more than a little like raw onion. All he cared about was that it was free. No matter how much these boring and un-adventurous Amish people turned up their noses at Fannie Graber's free food, he for one was going to eat as much as he could.

Nash watched Sarah through narrowed eyes. She had no idea he was watching her; she only had eyes for Benjamin. In fact, she stared at Benjamin throughout the whole meal. Nash prided himself on being observant, but even someone less observant than he could see Sarah Beachy was plainly head over heels in love with Benjamin Shetler, and what's more, was not happy that Benjamin was chatting with Jessie Yoder.

Nash smiled to himself. This was a golden opportunity. What's more, he was sure he could cause some trouble with Sarah's friend, Beth. He had no idea just what, but surely inspiration would strike him. His smirk widened.

Chapter Five

Beth was almost there. As the taxi turned onto a dirt road, the driver looked back and smiled. "I don't usually get too many calls out this way, but the property sure looks magnificent this time of year," he said, pointing out over the vast hillside covered in trees.

"Yes, it's lovely, just like I've been told," Beth said, looking out the window as they pulled up to the Millers' home. She was transfixed by the beautiful scenery.

"We're here, ma'am," the driver called out, pulling her attention back to reality.

"Sure." Beth fidgeted through her purse for money. After Beth paid for her trip, the driver unloaded her bags from the back of the taxi and placed them on the ground beside her.

As the driver turned to leave, another voice called out. "Ah, *gut!* You must be Beth, Sarah's friend. I'm Mr. Miller." The voice was warm and kind. When Beth turned toward its source, she saw a tall, older *mann* with a long, graying beard walking out from behind a large barn. "I'll help you with those bags— just follow me. My *fraa* has been eagerly waiting for you to arrive."

Beth smiled, happy to be with her friend's *familye* at last. "*Denki*," she said, following closely behind Mr. Miller as he carried her belongings up to the front door.

The door slowly opened to reveal a woman standing behind it. "I thought I heard some commotion out here. Has Beth finally arrived?" she asked, her voice full of excitement. "Come in! I've been cooking a meal all afternoon. The entire *familye* will be coming to dinner tonight just to meet you."

It had only been a matter of minutes since Beth arrived, and she already felt an innate sense of happiness. "I'm looking forward to meeting everyone," she said.

"I'm going to leave your things inside the room where you'll be staying," Mr. Miller said, pointing to the stairs. "I have some work I need to get finished before the guests arrive."

"*Denki*," was all Beth could muster before Mr. Miller had disappeared up the stairs.

Mrs. Miller motioned for Beth to follow her. "I'll show you around the *haus* and then take you to your room."

The house was even larger on the inside than it seemed on the outside, but it sure looked like a typical Amish home. It was modest, yet well-kept and spacious. The two floors offered plenty of extra rooms for guests and family, but the dining room was the one part of the house that stood out most. The large table in the center was lined with wooden chairs on all ends but one, where a large bench sat instead, no doubt made for young children to use.

"This room won't be this quiet soon," Mrs. Miller said, a hint of laughter in her voice. "Come this way, please."

Beth smiled, happy to be able to settle in and get ready for the upcoming dinner. When they reached the last room on the right, Mrs. Miller pushed open the door and headed inside. "This is where you'll be staying during your visit. Please make yourself at home while I finish up in the kitchen."

Beth nodded. "*Denki.*"

"The others will arrive soon, so enjoy the solitude while it lasts," Mrs. Miller said, before heading back to finish dinner.

Beth didn't have much in the way of belongings, but she unpacked her clothing and then made sure that she looked appropriate for the large get-together. As she focused on straightening her apron and fixing her prayer *kapp*, Sarah burst into the room.

"You're here!" she squealed.

Beth was overjoyed to see Sarah again. "Yes, I arrived not long ago. Your *familye* has been so warm and welcoming."

"Yes, they certainly are," Sarah said. "You might not have your own *familye* yet, but you'll always be a part of ours."

Beth nodded, unsure what to say. She knew Sarah

wasn't trying to bring forth sad thoughts, but the fact that she still hadn't been married was something that already followed her around like a dark cloud. Beth was in her mid-twenties after all, and most Amish women were married long before then.

"Still not having luck finding a good *mann*?" Sarah asked. Her voice was soft, but louder than a whisper.

"Unfortunately not," Beth replied, looking down at the linoleum. "I haven't been able to find a single one that's suitable."

"Well, don't let Mrs. Miller hear that! She seems to think that she's a wonderful matchmaker, but her taste in *menner* can be a bit unnerving. Anyway, let's go." Sarah laughed as she led Beth to the dining room.

Beth watched carefully as the countless faces came in and were introduced to her. She met Hannah, Esther, Martha, and their husbands, as well as Rebecca and Elijah. Beth thought the husbands all looked alike—but that was because three Miller *dochders* were married to three Hostetler *bruders*, and Rebecca was soon to marry the last Hostetler *bruder*. Beth hoped she would be able to remember everyone's names.

A small, plump woman was next to be introduced, but she introduced herself. "*Hiya*, I'm Mary," she pronounced, "and this is my David. We're to be married soon. David is the *sohn* of Mrs. Miller's *gut* friend, Beth Yoder. I live in the *grossmammi haus* by myself. I don't mind—I like the peace and quiet."

"There won't be peace and quiet when you marry

me," David said with a chuckle. "I'm sure we'll have lots of *bopplin*."

His face turned beet red after he spoke, as did Mary's. Beth resisted the urge to chuckle. They were such a sweet couple.

Mary cleared her throat and added, "This is David's *schweschder*, Jessie." She nodded to a sullen-faced girl.

"Good day," Jessie said without looking at Beth. She pulled out one of the wooden chairs and sat down hard on it.

"And I'm Beth Yoder," a woman said. "We share the same name."

Although the tone was warm, the younger Beth knew the older Beth was appraising her.

Jessie suddenly stood up, the length of the chair making a horrible scraping sound on the linoleum floor. "I'll show Beth around."

Everyone looked at Jessie in surprise. "Why would you want to show Beth around?" Mary asked her, her voice filled with suspicion.

Jessie did not respond, but simply walked over to Beth and took her by the arm. "I'll show you the barn," she said, and all but dragged Beth out of the house. Beth thought it a little strange, as she figured one barn looked pretty much like another barn. It was clear to her Mary thought Jessie had an agenda, but what could it possibly be?

When they reached the barn, the two women walked inside. "Those are the chickens," Jessie said in a bored tone.

It was all Beth could do not to say she had seen plenty of chickens in barns before. She looked at the chickens and then looked up, but to her surprise, Jessie was striding through the barn at a fast pace. Beth hurried after her, relishing the scent of hay, of horses, and of dust, a combination of scents much loved by the Amish and horse people but not usually enjoyed by others. To Beth, it was comforting and reassuring.

"We're going outside," Jessie said.

When they reached the back of the barn, Jessie leaned against a wooden fence. "It's been a boring afternoon so far," she said.

Beth was aware her jaw had fallen open in surprise at Jessie's rudeness.

Jessie was fiddling with her skirts and then produced something. Beth couldn't quite see what it was, but she was surprised by the fact that Jessie had sewn pockets into her skirts. Surely it must have been done to conceal something, but what?

She had the answer soon enough when Jessie lit a cigarette. Beth gasped.

Jessie blew smoke in her direction. "You're not going to tell, are you? I don't know you, but I didn't take you for a tattletale."

"Oh, no, no," Beth sputtered. "I won't tell."

The sides of Jessie's lips curled up ever so slightly. "That's *gut*. I *am* trying to break the habit. It's difficult." With that she took another long drag of the cigarette.

Beth realized she was staring, but she couldn't stop herself. She had never seen an Amish girl smoking before. Sure, she knew young people on *rumspringa* sometimes tried smoking, but she had never seen anyone Amish do it. "Does your mother know?" Beth finally asked.

"Yes," Jessie simply said.

"But wasn't she angry with you?"

"Yes," Jessie said, although this time, she smirked.

Beth was perplexed. "Well then, do you have a boyfriend? And does he mind?"

Jessie shrugged. "I don't have a boyfriend—yet. And I know you don't."

Beth's face fell. "*Nee*, I don't have a boyfriend."

Jessie waved one hand at her. "Don't worry about it. There's plenty of time. Don't let them push you into anything. That's my advice. Take it or leave it!"

"Um, thanks," Beth said. She was at a loss as to how to communicate with this girl, the strangest Amish girl she had ever met.

"We need to have a conversation," Jessie said.

Once more, Beth was perplexed. "Why?" she asked.

"Because my mother or that nosy Mrs. Miller will ask us what we were talking about," she said, "and we will need to give them an answer."

Beth scratched her head. "I see. So what will you and I have a conversation about?"

"I was hoping you'd have an idea," Jessie said.

"I'm not the one who is smoking and hiding the fact," Beth said. She was shocked that she had spoken so bluntly, but Jessie did not appear to mind.

"Fair enough," she said. "Let's talk about boys.

Mrs. Miller thinks that's all Amish girls talk about, anyway."

"Sure," Beth said. "What are the boys like in this community?"

Jessie pulled a face. "Boring. What are they like in your community?"

"Well, I'm not attracted to any of them," Beth said honestly.

"There's Benjamin Shetler who's just arrived in town and he's from another community," Jessie said. "It's obvious Sarah, your friend, likes him."

Benjamin! Benjamin Shetler? It was all Beth could do not to gasp. Was this why Sarah had summoned her? Sarah had written her that she had something important she needed to discuss with her, something about which she was quite upset, but she had not mentioned Benjamin's name. Had Benjamin come here looking for Sarah? Beth couldn't wait to find out.

"Do you know him?" Jessie snapped, shocking Beth out of her reverie.

"Oh, I was just thinking it strange that Sarah didn't mention anything to me given that I'm her friend," Beth said. She chose her words carefully so as not to lie to Jessie while still withholding information. To her relief, Jessie did not press the issue.

"I've just started working at the B&B where Rebecca Miller's been working," Jessie said. "Benjamin's been there a while, and the B&B is run by the Flickingers. You'll meet them soon. They have a son, Nash. He is English."

"He's English?" Beth said. This evening was bringing one surprise after another.

"I don't actually know if he's become English or whether he's just on a very long *rumspringa*," Jessie explained. "He's a bit of a wild one."

Beth detected a note of admiration in Jessie's voice. She wondered if Jessie liked Nash. Jessie's next words seemed to confirm her suspicions.

"You wouldn't be interested in him. None of the Amish girls would be. He says what he thinks and doesn't spare anyone's feelings, and he has tattoos and body piercings."

What sort of a community is this? Beth thought. "Do his parents mind?" she said when she finally found her voice.

Jessie nodded vigorously. "They sure do!"

"Oh," Beth said in a small voice.

Jessie threw her cigarette butt to the ground and stomped on it rather viciously with her boot. "Well, thanks for the conversation. Let's get back to the house. I'm starving." She rubbed her flat stomach.

They walked back to the house in silence until they had almost reached the stairs. Jessie pulled on Beth's arm. "Not so fast!"

She pulled Beth over to an herb garden where she broke off some peppermint leaves and rubbed them between her hands. She popped a few leaves in her mouth and chewed them rapidly.

It was almost dark now, and Beth thought Jessie was rather lucky. The peppermint was growing right next to the nettle, and Beth thought it wouldn't be too good if Jessie had grabbed a handful of nettle rather than peppermint.

"What are you doing that for?" she asked Jessie.

Jessie narrowed her eyes. "Obviously, it takes away the smell of the cigarettes," she said, her tone filled with derision.

And how on earth would I be expected to know that? Beth thought, but she kept silent.

When they walked back into the house, the first words out of Mrs. Miller's mouth were, "So what did you two girls talk about?"

"Told you so," Jessie whispered to Beth. In a louder voice, she said, "We were talking about boys."

Mrs. Miller clasped her hands with delight. "Well, we will soon have to find a nice husband for you, Jessie."

Beth noticed that Mrs. Yoder rubbed her brow. "I've been trying," she said and then shrugged.

Beth sympathized with her. She didn't know what sort of husband would suit Jessie Yoder. She sure wasn't the typical Amish girl. Beth also noticed that David and Mary were staring suspiciously at Jessie. Beth guessed they knew full well what Jessie had been doing.

When Beth moved away from Jessie and her overwhelming peppermint scent, she noticed the delicious aroma of good food. The dining table was laden with dinner.

Mrs. Miller indicated everyone should sit. Mr. Miller looked down, his eyes closed tightly. Beth closed her eyes for the traditional silent prayer, but this time also silently thanked *Gott* for the chance to spend time with such a lovely *familye*. When she opened her eyes, she saw bowls of mashed potatoes and gravy piled high beside dishes of creamed celery. Several trays of fresh bread lined the edges of the table as other various favorites laid scattered across the table top. There were desserts such as applesauce, cookies, and tapioca pudding, her favorite.

After the silent prayer, the dinner turned lively. Beth learned all about the Miller *schweschders*. She also learned more about the Hostetler *bruders*.

"So, when will your cousin be coming?" Mrs. Miller asked, her gaze set on Hannah's husband, Noah.

"He was supposed to be here by now," Noah replied.

"Noah, you're just like my husband, Abraham!" Mrs. Miller said in a scolding tone. "If you'd told me that before, we would not have started dinner without him! I don't know why the *menner* in this *familye* always see fit to withhold information from me. Why, I'm always the last to know!"

"Noah did tell you," Mr. Miller said with a chuckle. "I myself heard him."

"Oh well, I only ask because I'm excited for him to meet Beth. He is a lovely young *mann*. I think he and Beth would get along very well."

"*Mamm*, please! Beth doesn't need your matchmaking advice," Martha said, shaking her head. "Beth is here to visit with Sarah and spend time with us, not to find a *mann* to marry."

"I am aware of that, but what is wrong with trying to find a husband?" Mrs. Miller said, the volume of her voice rising.

"Nothing—except when it's you trying to make the match," Hannah added, causing all her *schweschders* to laugh quietly.

"Yes, pay her no mind," Rebecca said, earning a stare of disapproval from Mrs. Miller. "Or else you might regret it!"

Beth chuckled briefly before her mood turned somber once more. It was difficult being single, especially when others constantly pointed it out. She knew that they meant no harm, but she wasn't interested in any *menner* in her community.

Mrs. Miller cleared her throat loudly and addressed Hannah. "I knew you and Noah were meant for each other."

"*Mamm*, you did not. How can you forget all the trouble you caused me? It's a wonder Noah and I ever got married."

Mrs. Miller dismissed Hannah's remark with a wave of her cup, in the process losing her grip on the wide-rimmed cup's handle, and so spilling a drop or two of meadow tea. "I have a natural gift, I tell you. I was the one responsible for Hannah, Esther, and Martha marrying."

Mr. Miller was doing his best not to laugh. "Rachel, you said you were the one responsible for Naomi Reichenbach marrying Elam Zook. You said that's how it all started."

Mrs. Miller huffed. "I *was* responsible! It was

me! I did it. Now don't give me that look, Abraham, they've been very happy together for years now. Everyone said Elam Zook would never get married again after his wife went to be with *Gott*. I worked hard on that match for some time, if you recall. I invited them both for dinner many a time." Mrs. Miller looked as though she was about to explode, until Martha changed the subject.

"Anyway, Hannah, how's married life?"

"Martha, you ask me that every time I see you."

"That's because you always giggle strangely and blush."

"I don't giggle strangely, and I never blush," Hannah said, giggling and turning a shade of red that would make a beet envious.

Before Martha had a chance to respond to the remarks, a knock sounded through the house. "I think he's here," Noah said.

Mr. Miller leaped to his feet and left the room, only to return moments later with a tall, handsome man.

Is that the man Mrs. Miller is trying to set me up with? Beth wondered, recognizing the *mann* as single due to the fact he was clean-shaven. His handsome features accentuated a strong jaw line.

"I apologize for my tardiness," the man said.

"Beth, that's the man Mrs. Miller mentioned. He's the Hostetler *bruders*' cousin, Mark," Sarah said in a whisper.

As soon as she had realized who he was, Beth's heart sank to her stomach. *This* is Mark Hostetler?

Chapter Six

"*Hullo* Mark," Mr. Miller said, offering the man a warm smile. "You know most of the *familye*—but have you had the pleasure of meeting our guests? This is Sarah, and this is Mary. This is Beth, Sarah's friend, and she will be staying with us for a while."

"It's nice to meet you all," Mark said, his voice already grating on Beth's nerves.

After Beth sat there in a daze for a few moments, she finally acknowledged him by looking up and offering the most sincere smile that she could muster. She then stared coldly at the man whom she had only ever known by name, struggling with confusion. It couldn't be the same Mark Hostetler, though—could it? The man who had broken her friend's heart lived as far away from the Millers as she did, but was it possible that he was the very same person?

"We were worried that you weren't going to make it in time for dinner," Mrs. Miller said, looking over at Mark. "I hope your trip wasn't too troubling."

"Oh, it was fine, *denki*, Mrs. Miller." Mark walked over to the empty chair beside Noah and Hannah. "I got into town late this afternoon, but after tending to some business, I had to check in with Mr. and Mrs. Hostetler."

"That's right," Jacob said with a smile. "My *mudder* and my *vadder* would have been pleased to see you. We haven't seen you for ages."

It was beginning to dawn on Beth that he was most likely the same man she was hoping he wasn't, but if that was the case, then why? Why would Mrs. Miller be trying to set her up with someone so callous and inconsiderate?

Beth's thoughts turned to when her friend, Miriam Hilty, had told her she was engaged to that very man. Beth watched her friend go from blissfully happy to a broken husk of the woman that she used to be. The reasons he left her were still unknown to Beth, but what Miriam did tell her was how heartbroken and distraught Mark had made her. He had called off their marriage without warning, and disappeared shortly after. If Mark was indeed that same, awful man about whom Miriam had told her, then she wanted absolutely nothing to do with him.

When Beth looked up from her plate, she noticed everyone else had been locked in conversation while she was racking her brain about the newest dinner guest.

"How has business been, Mr. Miller?" Mark asked.

"The furniture business is doing well. My customers range from community members to many *Englischers*." Mr. Miller smiled from ear to ear.

"I'm glad to hear it," Mark said. Beth considered he looked much happier than he should after what he had done to Miriam.

"So, Mark, I see that you still haven't found a suitable *fraa*. How is that coming along?" Mrs. Miller asked. Her question was met with several gasps.

"Oh, well, I haven't really given that much thought since…well, since what happened before," Mark said.

Beth looked over at him with disgust. Was he talking about the day he had left her friend devastated and alone? What a horrible man he must truly be.

"Perhaps you should, then," Mrs. Miller continued. "And what about you, Beth?"

Beth sighed quietly before speaking. "There are very few eligible *menner* in my community," she said. "So, it just isn't something I've put too much thought into."

Sarah leaned over and whispered, "Pay her no mind. I knew she was going to do this."

Everyone at the table was so nice and welcoming to Mark. Yet did they know the type of man he actually was? It annoyed Beth to no end, as did the fact that Mrs. Miller seemed fairly relentless in her quest. It was an idea that did not sit well with her.

"Well, it's a *gut* thing there are other communities that do have *menner*," Mrs. Miller said, earning several glances from her daughters.

"I have no objections to finding a *fraa*, but work has been my primary focus of late," Mark said.

Mrs. Miller flashed him a wide smile. "It seems rather interesting that two single people have joined our large *familye* for dinner. Perhaps there could be something more to all of this."

Beth was still trying to avoid eye contact with Mark or Mrs. Miller, but she could feel the glaring heat of their stares, or at least that's what she thought.

They finally locked eyes but then Beth looked away. Beth's heart fluttered uncontrollably at the sight of Mark. He had a strong, commanding build, a pleasant face, and sparkling green eyes that seemed to reach into the depths of her being. She was annoyed with herself for being so pleasantly attracted to him.

Mrs. Miller was still talking. "Speaking of such things, why don't the two of you go fetch some fresh mint from the garden, so that I can make some mint tea? There's a basket in the kitchen you can use." Mrs. Miller pointed to the kitchen door.

Beth glanced up at Mark at about the same time he turned toward her. Not only did she have to look all throughout dinner at the man who hurt her friend, but now she was being forced to spend some time with him alone. It would be rude to turn Mrs. Miller down, but it took all the will power she could muster not to object.

Mark stood up and turned to Beth. "Shall we?"

With a quick nod, Beth rose and followed him out of the room. The discussion picked right back up the moment they left, causing her to feel even more trapped and helpless. She was now alone with someone who didn't deserve even a minute of her time, not after all the pain he had caused. And why did she feel so attracted to him when she knew the sort of man he was?

As they walked out the front door and headed toward the herb garden a short distance from the main house, Beth found herself focusing her thoughts on anything other than her current situation. The last thing that she wanted to do was clue him in on how she truly felt right then.

"So, I take it you're new to these parts," Mark said, flashing a smile that almost looked welcoming. "Do you visit the Millers often?"

"I hadn't before, but Sarah wanted me to spend some time with her."

"It seems that many Amish are relocating to larger communities around these parts," Mark said, kneeling down before a large mint plant.

Beth stared at Mark. He had broken her friend's heart. Beth couldn't find it in herself to be so brash and mention it to him, but she also couldn't shake the thought from her mind. It was almost humorous how he didn't seem to have a clue that she was a friend of Miriam's. Beth was sure that he had at least heard of her name as she had his, but from the looks of it, he had yet to put two and two together.

Beth noticed that the basket was almost full already, and she hadn't even lifted a finger to help.

Mark was already back on his feet. "I think this is plenty of mint for some tea."

"Yes, that looks like a good amount," she said dryly.

"Then let's head back to dinner," Mark said with a smile.

The walk back to the main house wasn't a long one, but the dead silence that hung over them the entire way was rather unbearable. Beth wanted nothing more than to be away from Mark's side, but from the way he kept glancing at her, she could tell that he was forming his own opinions of her as well.

As they approached the door, Mark held it open for her, still flashing smiles here and there and being as kind as could be. It was confusing for Beth, but that was something that deceitful people did all the time, wasn't it? Didn't they tend to try to make themselves look so sweet and caring when they weren't?

When the pair returned to dinner, Mrs. Miller immediately addressed them. "You're back so soon? What did you both think of each other?"

"I didn't think we should hold up dinner any longer than I already have," he said, extending the basket toward her.

"I appreciate the sentiment," Mrs. Miller said, "but you could have at least taken some time to talk and get to know each other." She glanced at Beth and Mark in turn as she spoke. "What made that sound?"

"What sound?" Mary and Rebecca said in unison.

"Is it your cat, Sarah?" Mrs. Miller continued.

Sarah looked at her cat. He was curled up, fast asleep on a cushion. "*Nee*, it's not my cat."

"There's the noise again," Mrs. Miller insisted. "Can't anyone else hear it?"

Just then, Beth heard a plaintive meow coming from the door.

Chapter Seven

"It looks like someone might have left her here," Mark said, crouching down beside the large box.

"Who would have done such a thing? And why?" Mary asked, scratching her forehead. "Pirate was abandoned too."

As Beth watched on, she saw Mark was still trying to console the kitten. "It's okay, little kitten. I won't hurt you," he said quietly, extending his hand toward the frail little kitten and gently petting its head. The kitten snuggled into him.

Why would the kitten act like that to him of all people? From what Miriam had told her, Mark Hostetler was a cruel, cold man with no affections toward anyone or anything. That sure didn't seem to be the case right then, but other than what she had been told, Beth had no idea what to believe.

"The poor thing looks like it hasn't eaten in ages," Sarah said, shaking her head.

"That could very well be, or the kitten could be

sick," Mrs. Miller said, her voice getting louder as she spoke. "Either way, perhaps someone should take the poor little thing to the veterinarian. Can somebody please call a taxi?"

"Yes, I'll call right now from my workshop," Mr. Miller said, before hurrying down the front steps.

As he darted off toward the large building, Mrs. Miller's voice pulled Beth's attention back to the porch. "Mark, perhaps you and Beth should take this kitten to see the vet. It seems trusting of only you so far, and it would be unseemly to send you on your own."

Beth's chest tightened. Was this another part of Mrs. Miller's plan to match them up?

"I could go with Mark," Sarah said, raising her eyebrows at Beth.

Mrs. Miller shook her head. "*Nee*, Beth should accompany Mark." Her voice was firm.

Beth knew right then that resistance was pointless, but the kitten did look to be in need of help, and after all, how bad could a trip to the veterinarian really be? Even if she had to listen to Mark's grating voice the entire trip, at least it would placate Mrs. Miller and get the little kitten back to good health. Two good outcomes were worth a long ride into town with anyone, even the man who had broken her friend's heart, or at least that's what she was telling herself. "I don't mind going. It's just that I had planned to help clean up after dinner."

"Don't you worry about that," Mrs. Miller said, her voice stern. "It will all be cleaned up by the time you and Mark return with the kitten." She glanced down at the cat now nestled in Mark's arms.

Beth had been right; resistance really was pointless. Beth flashed the woman the most sincere smile she could muster before walking away and turning to Sarah. "Is this another part of Mrs. Miller's matchmaking scheme?" she whispered.

"I'm sure it is, but you don't really have to go if you don't want though," Sarah said with a frown.

"It's okay. I would just like to know what is going on. Where did that kitten even come from?"

"I'm not sure, but Mark seems to love her," Sarah said, nodding toward Mark.

When Beth looked over, she saw him still holding the kitten. Beth stared at Mark, thinking it all a little odd. He seemed caring and nurturing. Something seemed wrong, but Beth couldn't hold back her irritation. Miriam had been her friend for a long time, albeit not a close one, but to know that a man could break her heart without any remorse was too much for her.

Moments later, Mr. Miller returned to the porch where the entire *familye* was still gathered. "The taxi will be here soon," he said, as he climbed the steps toward the others.

And he was right, because the taxi showed up just minutes later. The screeching tires drew up some dirt in the yard, but since it was getting late and the kitten needed to be seen by a veterinarian, nobody seemed to mind.

"Come along, Beth," Mark said, making his way over to the car.

As she climbed into the back seat, she overheard Mark asking the driver to take them to the veterinary hospital in town. Mark sat down beside her, still holding the silent kitten gently. "It sure has been a strange day, hasn't it?"

"Yes, although I can't say that is a *gut* thing. If it weren't for that cute little critter, this day would all but be over already. It's bothersome."

Mark's forehead furrowed as he looked back at her. "I suppose that's true, but days are usually more happy than bothersome."

Beth was frustrated. "It's not the days that are bothersome," she said, shaking her head before looking away. The trees passed by so quickly that all she could see out her window was a blur of colors. The view was hardly entertaining, but anything that would keep her attention away from Mark and keep him from talking to her would suffice.

"Oh, well then I hope that whatever ails you will go away," Mark said, his voice softer.

"I hope so too," Beth said, refusing to look back at him.

Before she knew it, the taxi was coming to a stop. The driver turned to them. "We're here." He extended his hand for the money.

Mark at once paid him.

"Thank you," the driver said, in his deep, raspy voice. "Shall I wait?"

"We'll call for another when we're finished," Mark replied, "but thank you as well."

"Take care!" the *Englischer* said, turning back around in his seat.

As they stepped out into the chilly evening, Beth watched the cab drive away. When she turned back to the building, Mark was already standing in the doorway, clutching the kitten to his chest and propping the door open for her. "Are you coming?"

"*Jah*," she said, hurrying up the steps.

The lobby was empty when they walked in, but a plump, outgoing woman with a happy smile on her face sat at the main desk. "Good evening. Is there something I can help you two with? Oh, look at her. She's adorable. Poor thing looks like she's nearly starved though." The woman stood up.

"We were having dinner with *familye* and friends, and we heard this kitten at the door. We assume she's a stray, or maybe someone abandoned her," Mark explained.

"I see. Let me get you registered in the system, and as soon as the doctor's ready, we'll help get your kitten back to health." The receptionist handed Mark a form.

The pair went and sat in the waiting room, but Beth's tension wouldn't seem to fade. Beth couldn't even look over at Mark without feeling a sense of anger. It was troubling her to feel such a way, but if he had no remorse over what he did to Miriam, then why should she feel bad about how she had been acting toward him? The conflict was unsettling, but by the time the veterinarian called their names, she had managed to avoid talking to him at all as they sat waiting.

They followed the vet back to a small room with a large, metal table in the center. "Could you please put her down here?" the vet asked Mark.

He gently placed the kitten on the table. As the vet inspected the kitten, Mark looked over at Beth and flashed a half-hearted smile. She wasn't sure what he meant by it, but if he felt badly about something, then it was all on him. She had been as kind and respectful as possible, despite the way she felt about him.

"So, it looks as though she's completely fine," the vet said, smiling as she petted the kitten softly. "She just needs some good nutrition. She clearly hasn't been getting the vitamins and minerals kittens need to grow and mature and be healthy. If you're interested, we have a special kind of food that will get her back to a healthy weight rather quickly."

"That sounds great," Mark said. "This food will make her feel better?"

"It will do that and much more," the vet replied. "That should be all she'll need for now, since I've just given her a worming tablet and her first vaccination."

"Great, then I'll take a large bag of it," he said.

Beth was immediately taken aback by the gesture, nearly gasping out loud. Why would he care so much about a random kitten that had been left on the porch? Considering how callous he had been toward her friend, it made little sense that he would be acting in such a manner now. What was going on?

After the veterinarian had finished her paperwork,

she led them back to the lobby where the products were kept. "This would be your best bet, but the price is a bit steep. It should last you quite a while though. Here, let's see if she likes it. We have samples to try."

The woman turned toward the kitten, now wrapped in Mark's arms again, and extended a handful of the food to her. The kitten ate the food greedily.

"Looks like I'll take it," Mark said, smiling as he glanced over at Beth. "And do you have a phone I can use to call a taxi?" he asked the vet.

"Yes, certainly."

The taxi arrived about ten minutes later, but it was now quite late in the evening. Mark put the cat food onto the seat and then climbed in beside Beth before they headed back to the Millers' *haus*. He looked happy, and that made her even more upset.

Sarah couldn't wait for the opportunity to speak with Beth in private. There was only so much one could write in letters, and Sarah had missed her friend dearly. As the night drew on, Sarah could see Beth yawning widely. She hoped Beth wouldn't be too tired to speak with her as she had waited so long for the opportunity.

Finally, all the guests left, and Mary went back to her *grossmammi haus*. Rebecca too made her excuses and retired for the night.

Sarah grabbed Beth's arm. "At last! I've been so desperate to tell you everything that's happened. Are you too tired to try to talk tonight?" she asked after Beth yawned widely once more.

Beth waved her concerns away. "*Nee*, I'm fine. I've been in suspense. You didn't tell me Benjamin Shetler was here!"

Sarah looked around the room, even though she knew everyone had gone to bed. Her fat ginger cat, Tom, was asleep on Mrs. Miller's favorite chair. Sarah smiled. Tom wouldn't do that if Mrs. Miller was awake. "Let's talk in the kitchen," she said. "Fancy some hot chocolate?"

"*Jah*, that might help keep me awake," Beth said.

"Are you sure you're not too tired?" Sarah asked again.

"*Nee*, I'm fine. I'll feel better after some hot chocolate."

Sarah put some brown sugar, cocoa, and a little water in a saucepan and stirred it until it bubbled.

"Your hot chocolate is the best," Beth said. "I've missed you, Sarah."

"I've missed you too," Sarah said. She poured in some milk, maple syrup, and then five large marshmallows. She stirred them in for a few moments and decided to add another five marshmallows for good measure.

When the girls were sitting, each with a large mug of steaming, sweet hot chocolate, Beth tapped one finger on the table. "Now, out with it, Sarah! Why didn't you tell me Benjamin Shetler was here?"

Sarah shook her head. "He hasn't been here that long. I wanted to tell you in person. Thanks so much for coming."

"Of course I would come," Beth said. "So what's

happening between the two of you? Is *anything* happening between you?"

Sarah sighed and looked into her cocoa. "*Nee.* Nothing's changed."

Beth threw up her hands. "Then why is he here?" She must have realized she had spoken too loudly, as she clamped her hand over her mouth. "Sorry," she said in a whisper. "If he doesn't like you, then why is he here?"

"Because my father sent him to fetch me."

Beth gasped. "He did?"

Sarah nodded slowly. "I'm afraid so."

"And do you know who your real father is yet?"

Sarah rubbed her eyes, hoping that would forestall the tears that were threatening to fall. "*Nee.* I still don't have a clue."

"Are you sure Benjamin isn't interested in you?"

Sarah shrugged. "Sometimes I think he is, but he's never once asked me on a buggy ride. Besides, I can't trust him. He's doing my father's wishes. After all, my father sent him here to fetch me back home. What's more, he went straight to the Flickingers' B&B nearby—he didn't come here and make himself known. He was here for a few days before I even found out about it."

Beth shook her head. "*Nee,* that isn't good."

Sarah pinched her forehead with one hand. "It's giving me a headache. I don't know what I can do about it."

"It doesn't seem that there *is* anything you can do about it, surely?"

"I'm not going back home to my stepfather," Sarah said. "I need answers. I need to find out who my real father is. Why won't anyone tell me?"

Beth leaned over and patted Sarah's hand. "I'm sorry."

Sarah decided to change the subject, at least until she knew she was in no danger of bursting into tears. "So, what did Jessie Yoder want to speak with you about?"

Beth bit her lip. She had promised Jessie she wouldn't tell anyone, but Sarah was her closest friend. "Well, I'd like to tell you, but I told Jessie I wouldn't tell anyone."

"Oh, so she used you as her cover story to smoke a cigarette."

Beth looked up sharply, causing Sarah to laugh. "Don't worry, Beth. Everybody knows Jessie smokes. She goes around reeking of a mixture of peppermint and cigarette smoke."

Beth chuckled. "She's the most unusual person I've ever met."

"You wait until you meet Nash Grayson," Sarah said with a laugh.

"Is he more unusual than Jessie?" Beth said, yawning once more.

Sarah pulled a face. "You just wait and see. Beth, I only made enough cocoa for one mug each. Would you like some more?"

Beth said that she would, so Sarah went back to the stove and put some brown sugar, cocoa, and water into a pot.

"How do you feel about Benjamin?" Beth said. "I know what you said in your letters, but has anything changed?"

"I've always felt the same way about him," Sarah said, stirring the pot. She went on and on, pouring out her feelings about Benjamin in a heartfelt manner. After she stirred in more marshmallows, she turned around. Beth was fast asleep, her head on the kitchen table. Her mouth was open and she was snoring ever so gently.

Chapter Eight

Nash Grayson was quite pleased with himself. He was in the buggy driven by Benjamin Shetler and they were heading to the Yoders' farm. For a start, Nash was looking forward to seeing Jessie Yoder, and he was also looking forward to meeting Beth, Sarah's friend. Surely he could cause some trouble there, but as yet he had no idea what it would be. Nevertheless, the opportunity excited him. What's more, he knew he got on Benjamin's nerves, so he was delighted to spend time with him.

"How much further is it?" he asked Benjamin.

"Pretty much the same as it was the last time you asked, a minute ago," Benjamin said.

Nash laughed. "Aren't all you Amish supposed to be patient and forbearing and everything else?"

Benjamin merely grunted.

"So how far is it again?" Nash asked.

Benjamin simply ignored him.

"That was good of the Flickingers to lend you their

buggy," Nash said. "This is a good horse. I helped choose him at the auction. The only thing is, he's quite slow."

"Good," was Benjamin's only response.

When they finally reached the Yoders' farm, Nash saw that the others had already arrived. Mary, Sarah, and David were throwing sticks to Pirate in the yard. Nash craned his neck to look for Jessie, but there was no sign of her or of her mother, Beth Yoder.

As soon as Benjamin stopped the buggy, Nash jumped out, leaving Benjamin to tend to the horse. He walked over to the group and flashed a wide smile.

Sarah made the introductions. "Beth, this is Nash Grayson, the Flickingers' son. Nash, this is my good friend, Beth."

"Another Beth," Nash said. "I always say the Amish should not be so conservative with names. What do they think would happen if they used a good, non-boring name? Would they go to hell for having names that aren't boring?" He thought he had gone a little far with the boring remark, so quickly added, "Not that Beth is a boring name. It's a nice name. It just gets confusing when there are five people in the same room and they are all called 'Beth.' It would be less confusing if your parents named you Arabella, or Gertrude, or even Mildred."

Nash noticed with satisfaction that Beth was staring at him, her mouth wide open. He had taken out his piercings and worn a long-sleeved shirt to cover his tattoos. Maybe he should have left in the piercings to give Beth an even bigger shock, but he wanted to keep on the good side of Mrs. Yoder. Not that he figured he was on her good side at the moment, but he certainly didn't want to get on her bad side. He figured she could be a real mean, even more so than Mrs. Miller.

Nash noticed that Sarah and Benjamin were avoiding looking at each other. He made a mental note of that, and he also noticed how Beth was keenly staring from Sarah to Benjamin and back again. It was clear to Nash that Beth knew all about Sarah and Benjamin. Still, that was to be expected given they were close friends.

Beth could scarcely believe her eyes when she saw Nash Grayson. She couldn't see the tattoos or the piercings that Sarah had mentioned. She figured he had removed his piercings for the visit to the Yoders' farm and figured his shirts were concealing his tattoos. She could now see what Sarah meant about him—he certainly did speak his mind and what he said wasn't terribly nice. She thought him rather rude, but he certainly was an attractive man, tall with dark hair. Still, his attitude was objectionable and he was rather too full of himself. She didn't think English girls would like him for that reason, although they would no doubt be attracted to him for his looks.

Beth Yoder appeared behind the group, her "*Hullo*," starting Beth.

Beth swung around. "*Hullo* again, Mrs. Yoder."

"And how is that kitten you found?" Mrs. Yoder asked.

"She's *gut*," Beth said and silently added, *How would I know? Mark won't let her out of his sight.*

"And where is Mark Hostetler?" Mrs. Yoder asked her.

Beth shrugged. "I don't know. I assume he's helping the Millers, although I didn't see him this morning."

Nash pricked up his ears. Why was Mrs. Yoder asking Beth in particular how Mark Hostetler was? He hadn't met Mark Hostetler, but he imagined he was a do-gooder like the rest of the Hostetlers. Still, he noticed Beth was somewhat uneasy at the mention of him. Had she perhaps developed a little crush on him? Or was Mrs. Yoder simply going over the top with her matchmaking efforts with the encouragement of her good friend, Mrs. Miller?

"I'll just go for a walk and stretch my legs," Nash said. "My parents' horse is very slow, so it took us a long time to get here and I'm cramped." With that, he walked off in the direction of the barn. He figured Jessie was either in the house helping or she was behind the barn, no doubt doing something nefarious.

He was right. He could smell cigarette smoke as he approached a bush. "Oh look, it's a burning bush and I'm not even Moses," he said. "Maybe there's a message for me from above."

Jessie stood up. "Very funny," she said. "You'd better watch out, Nash. You're showing off your Bible knowledge."

"Exodus, chapter three," Nash said smugly.

Jessie ground her cigarette under her boot. "And I never thought I'd be calling you of all people *Scripture Smart*."

"Well, I came here with Benjamin Shetler, and Sarah and her friend Beth are here."

Jessie shrugged one shoulder. "I've already met Beth."

"What's she like?"

Jessie narrowed her eyes. "Why do you ask?" Her tone held suspicion.

"Just curious."

Jessie looked him up and down before answering. "She is no worse than the rest of them."

"It seems that your mother is trying to matchmake her with Mark Hostetler."

"Are you jealous?" Jessie asked him. "Do you want her for yourself?"

Nash smirked. "No I don't, but are you jealous?"

He thought Jessie would be annoyed, but she simply laughed and pulled another cigarette from her skirt before lighting it. She took a long deep breath and blew a long stream of smoke in Nash's direction. "You should be so lucky," she said slowly. "Anyway, you had better get back to the others or they will look for you and find me."

Nash was going to say something but thought the better of it. "Fine," he said.

Beth looked in horror as Mark Hostetler approached in the Millers' gray top buggy. She had been looking forward to a pleasant morning, not one where she had to endure the company of such a man as he.

"Are you all right?" Sarah asked her. "Clearly Mrs. Miller's motives for sending the two of us there today with Mary was to matchmake us," she added in a whisper.

"*Jah*, I'm all right," Beth said, not altogether truthfully. She figured Sarah would think she was attracted to Mark and thus nervous. She wished she could tell Sarah what Miriam had told her about Mark, but Miriam had sworn her to secrecy. Beth didn't like to keep anything from Sarah, but she could not betray Miriam's trust, and so she had to keep the news to herself.

Still, Beth figured Mrs. Miller would have been right if Mark had been a good, honest person. The two of them did seem like a good match. Beth was only too painfully aware she was way past the usual Amish age for marriage, and Mark Hostetler would seem a most pleasant sort of man to someone who didn't know the truth about him.

Mark jumped down from the buggy all too cheerfully. *It's easy for him to be cheerful when he's broken the heart of my friend*, Beth thought with dismay.

Mrs. Yoder greeted him joyfully. "Come inside, all of you. I have some wet bottom Shoo-fly pie for you all and some garden tea, and Mrs. Graber kindly left us a plate of anchovy cream pie." She chuckled as she said it.

"I'll have it, if no one else will," Nash said.

Beth noticed that everyone sighed with relief. "What's in anchovy cream pie?" she asked.

"I'll save you a piece so you can see for yourself," Nash said, his eyes narrowed.

"Well then, go inside, all of you." Mrs. Yoder made shooing motions with her hands as if she were herding some recalcitrant chickens.

Everyone walked into the house—everyone that is, except David and Mary, who stayed outside with Pirate. Beth figured they wanted some alone time.

"It's nice to see you two again," Mrs. Yoder said, addressing her remark to Beth and Mark. "It's so unusual to have two single people visit our community at the same time."

Sarah and Beth exchanged glances.

"So, Sarah and Benjamin, have you had much time to get acquainted?" Mrs. Yoder continued. "I know I said two single people have recently arrived in the community, but four people have arrived! *Der Herr* certainly does work in mysterious ways. It's unusual to have a visitor to our community, but four visitors in a short space of time, and each one of them single!" She smiled widely.

Sarah felt awfully awkward around Benjamin. She had no idea he would be going to the Yoders' farm. Had Mrs. Miller arranged it? She wasn't sure. Her heart sank to her stomach. Surely she and Benjamin would not be able to keep up the façade, pretending they didn't know each other. Someone was sure to find out. She was certain the bishop's wife, Fannie Graber knew, and she wondered how good she was keeping secrets.

Sarah noted that Benjamin also looked uncomfortable and squirmed in his seat. *Serve him right*, she thought. *It's not good that he's here to try to make me return home*. She glared at Benjamin. At that time, he looked up and met her eyes, and then looked away at once. Sarah felt ashamed, but then set her resolve. *I haven't done anything wrong. He's the one who has done something wrong*, she thought. She looked up to see Mrs. Yoder studying her carefully.

Mrs. Yoder was still talking. "Well Mark, I hope you enjoy your time here."

"*Denki*, Mrs. Yoder," he said. "I *am* enjoying my time with the Miller *familye*."

"And how are you enjoying your time at the Flickingers' B&B?" Mrs. Yoder asked Benjamin.

"It's *wunderbar*," he said, although his tone did not match his words.

Just then Jessie Yoder entered the room, the strong scent of peppermint wafting before her. "Is there any Shoo-fly pie left for me?" she asked.

"Yes, help yourself," her mother said.

Sarah wondered if Mrs. Yoder would try to matchmake her daughter with Benjamin or Mark, or whether she had given her up as a lost cause.

"Come and sit with us, Jessie," said Mrs. Yoder said. "Benjamin, have you seen much of my *dochder* now she is working at the B&B?"

Sarah noted Nash was fidgeting. *Surely Nash isn't interested in Jessie?* Sarah wondered. *He is no longer Amish, but then again, Jessie is not your typical Amish girl.*

Benjamin shot Jessie a wide smile. "Yes, we have run into each other on occasion."

Sarah was discomforted. *Surely Benjamin can't be interested in Jessie?* Sarah thought with concern. A sharp pang of jealousy assaulted her and she shook her head to clear her thoughts. *What's wrong with me?* she thought and then squirmed in her seat when she saw Mrs. Yoder staring at her.

"Oh Mark, how rude of me," Mrs. Yoder continued. "I forgot you hadn't met my daughter yet. This is Jessie. Jessie, this is Mark Hostetler, the Hostetler *bruders'* cousin. You met years ago when you were both *kinner.*"

Jessie looked Mark up and down. Sarah thought she looked like a cat waiting to pounce. "*Hiya,*" Jessie said curtly.

"*Hiya,*" Mark responded rather more pleasantly.

Sarah hoped Mark wasn't interested in Jessie, because she thought he would be a good match for Beth. After all, everyone knew what a lovely *familye* the Hostetlers were and she really wanted Beth to be settled in a good marriage and have *kinner.*

To her relief, Mark didn't seem too keen on Jessie, but his eyes kept darting to Beth. That pleased Sarah. She carefully watched Benjamin as much as she could without overtly staring at him, and to her relief, his eyes did not wander to Jessie at any point. Still, she noticed that Nash Grayson seemed rather taken with Jessie. As Sarah watched, she saw Jessie shooting glances at Nash from time to time.

Now they'd be a good match, Sarah thought with

amusement, *only Nash would have to go back to the Amish, and I don't know what the bishop would think about that.* She silently reprimanded herself. Of course, anyone would be welcomed back to the Amish if they wanted to return to the community, but then again, would Nash want to return to the community? He certainly seemed to be enjoying the English lifestyle rather too much.

Chapter Nine

The gentle sounds of the morning awoke Beth just before the crack of dawn. Beth had suffered the worst night's sleep she had ever experienced. Her head was thumping, and it hurt as it had never hurt before. She put her hands to her head in an effort to will it to stop hurting. She wasn't sure whether it was a simple headache, or maybe all her thinking had caused the pain in her head.

Could there be another Mark Hostetler? Could there be two men with the same name? Surely not, the Millers had mentioned the community he was from. It was the same Mark Hostetler all right, as much as Beth didn't want to accept the fact. There was just no escaping it. No amount of wishful thinking in the whole world could change it.

Beth sat up, rubbing the weariness from her eyes as a wonderful aroma filled the house. Someone was brewing *kaffi*. Ready to start the day, she headed down to the kitchen, fully expecting to find Mrs.

Miller, Rebecca, Mary, or Sarah there—but she was wrong. It was Mark.

"Good morning!" he said, holding a mug to his lips. "I made some *kaffi* for everyone and fried some liver pudding. You're welcome to join me."

Beth just stood there, her arms dangling by her sides as she stared at him. What was he doing participating in women's work? In all her years, she had not once met an Amish *mann* who would do such a thing. He was the first, and probably the last, that she would ever know. Before she could comment on his transgressions, however, Mrs. Miller's voice pierced the temporary silence of the room.

"What is going on here?" she said, her eyes fixated on Mark and the mug of *kaffi* in his hands.

"*Guten mariye*, Mrs. Miller. I was up before everyone else so I didn't think it would cause any harm if I were to brew some *kaffi* and fry some liver pudding for all of us," he said, his voice gentle.

"Well, you must be one of those new Amish then, because that is just not acceptable. Your work is out in the fields, the shops, and where needed otherwise, but the *haus* is where women work. Sure, *menner* need to know how to cook in case their *fraa* is sick, but it just won't do on other occasions. I'll forgive it this time, but please try to adhere to propriety, at least as long as you're staying with us," she replied in a strict tone.

"Yes, of course, Mrs. Miller. I apologize for my misstep." Mark looked down at the floor as though ashamed.

Beth watched on quietly, wondering what was

going on with him. Why was Mark going so far out of his way to seem kind and caring, especially if it meant forgoing tradition? It made no sense to her, so all Beth could do was shake her head before walking back toward her room. The *kaffi* had been tempting, but her disgust for what that *mann* had done to Miriam had taken away any sense of appetite she had, even her desire for *kaffi*.

Beth, Sarah, and Mary spent the morning doing laundry. "*Denki* for your help," Mrs. Miller said. "I am going to start lunch, so I will see you shortly," she added, before heading off to the kitchen.

After Mrs. Miller had left the room, Beth shook her head and nearly laughed. "Yes, you might want to start lunch before Mark does."

"Before Mark does what?" a familiar voice asked.

Turning around in a sudden state of shock, Beth could feel her skin warming as she looked back at Mark Hostetler. "I'm sorry. I didn't mean to sound rude."

"Oh, well, I can't say that you accomplished that feat, but no harm's done," he said, stroking the little kitten as she lay nestled in his arm.

"What are you still doing with that cat?" she asked, confused by his fondness for the little kitten after what Miriam had said about him. "We still don't even know where she came from."

"Yes, but what does that matter? She needs a home and a loving *familye*, and I believe it's already been said that she trusts me," he said.

Beth could feel her chest tightening as the irritation finally struck a nerve. The kitten was only trusting of him because he was the first to hold her, and because he wouldn't let anyone else get close to her. What was he trying to prove? "That might be the case, but you can't just force others to like you."

Beth was momentarily alarmed at the way her voice sounded, at the way she'd spoken so harshly to Mark. She heard Sarah gasp from the other side of the room. She knew that she had sounded like a squawking, angry bird, but at that moment she didn't care a toss. Beth's heart was pounding, and the pounding was going to her head. What possible excuse could he have for the way he had treated Miriam Hilty? Certainly none that she could think of.

Mark walked over toward the fireplace. He placed the kitten gently on the chair beside it and then worked at getting a fire started. Beth stood there, glaring at him. "Is it really cold enough for a fire? It's still rather early."

Mark picked up the kitten, cradled her in his arms, and sat by the fire. After a few minutes had gone by, he slowly glanced up at Beth and smiled. "I'm sorry, but she was getting cold. I can't just let her freeze because it's warm enough for us."

How absurd! Why was he pretending to be someone he certainly was not? Mark appeared to be nothing like the *mann* she had pictured from Miriam's words, but how much of it was a façade? She normally would never think such a thing of Amish *menner*, but he wasn't very similar to them at all. There was something odd about Mark, and the anger burning inside Beth made it difficult for her to think rationally around him.

"Well, then, I hope she is feeling better now, but not everyone is so trusting after a good deed or two," she said, turning away and heading toward the kitchen to be rid of him.

"Mrs. Miller, would you happen to need any help with lunch? I could set the table if you'd like," Beth said, hoping to find solace in some extra work.

"That would be fine. I'm making a pot pie, so you're welcome to prepare the vegetables while I finish these noodles. They're over on the countertop waiting to be cleaned and cut. I had Mr. Miller fetch them from the root cellar before he went back to work," she said, her attention never leaving the steaming pot before her. "I was thinking of making a Shoo-fly pie as well, but we will save that for dinner."

Beth smiled, even though the woman couldn't see it. She was just happy to be away from Mark, even if it was only for a short time. Being around him made her feel a bit awkward, but she couldn't quite put her finger on what was causing that sensation. Was it solely because of the heartbreak he had caused her friend, or was it now mixed with the strange way that he had been acting since showing up? If he wasn't such a horrible *mann*, she would have been attracted to him. Shrugging that disturbing thought from her mind, Beth pulled some fresh vegetables from the refrigerator and washed them in the sink.

As the afternoon quickly approached, Beth finished preparing the vegetables and then headed to set the dining table for the meal. She placed the plates around it, but as she went to lay the last one down, the grating voice startled her once more. "Would you like some help with that?" Mark asked, his voice quiet enough so Mrs. Miller would not hear.

"You cannot be serious." Beth shook her head as she averted eye contact with him. "Anyway, I thought that kitten was cold. Why did you take the poor thing away from the fire?"

Mark paused, his eyes narrowing as she finally looked back at him. "Why did I take her away from the fire? Perhaps it's because she is no longer shivering in my arms. I know what I'm doing, regardless of how you may perceive me."

"I just don't understand why you keep trying to help around the kitchen, even after being asked not to. I have work to do, however," Beth said. She walked back into the kitchen. "The table is prepared. Would you like me to start rolling the flour for the crust?" Beth asked Mrs. Miller, but moments later, Mark was back.

"I just need to feed the kitten," he said, making his way toward the small cabinet where the dishes were kept. Seconds later, he pulled out a small bowl and placed it on the floor. "That should do the trick."

Beth wondered whether Mark really wanted to feed the kitten. It seemed more like he was just trying to be nosy. Either way, his scheme was really beginning to annoy her.

"I see that you and the kitten are rather fond of each other," Mrs. Miller said.

"I believe we are," he said, patting the kitten gently. "I'm thinking that we should name her soon."

"Perhaps you should be the one to name her," Mrs. Miller said. "Since we found that kitten, you've clearly shown her the most care of anyone. For that reason, I think she should be yours."

"Really?" Mark said, swallowing hard. "I can keep her?"

"I don't see why anyone would object. And besides, she might keep you busy enough where you won't feel the need to partake in women's work again," she said, a hint of laughter in her voice. "Although she didn't stop you this morning, did she?"

"She nearly did, but you're right. I promise never to make that mistake again while staying with you, Mrs. Miller."

Moments earlier, Beth's skin had been warm with anger, but now she only felt cold. She might not have been as overly affectionate to the kitten as Mark had been, but that was because he hadn't let the little kitten out of his sight since she had arrived on the porch. Because of that, there was no way for anyone else could have bonded with her.

"I just have one question. We don't even know where the kitten came from," Beth said, hoping to bring forth an objection without overtly appearing to do so. "What if she strayed from her home and a *familye* is looking for her?"

"I don't see how that could even be possible," Mark said, irritating Beth even further. "The poor little kitten was starving. It's not every day that a helpless animal finds its way to your door."

"I just meant that she might not be yours to claim." Beth let out a long, drawn-out sigh. Mark was the most irritating man she had ever met.

Chapter Ten

"Are you almost ready?" Sarah called to Beth from right outside her bedroom.

"Yes, I'll just be a minute," she replied, quickly tying her bonnet before opening the door. "I'm ready now."

"I didn't mean to rush you. It's just that the *menner* are already waiting outside in the buggy for us." Sarah motioned for Beth to follow her out.

As they walked outside and climbed down the steps, Beth paused and turned to her friend. In a whisper, she asked, "Is it really necessary for him to come?"

Sarah stopped, her brows furrowed. "Mark? Of course it is. Mrs. Ramseyer needs all the help around the house that she can get—inside and out. Why wouldn't we bring him?"

"Oh, it's just that I didn't know how much help he'd be," Beth said, looking away with a sense of shame after realizing that she was close to saying too much.

"Well, if it means that Benjamin won't be alone to cut the firewood and stack it in the shed, then that's reason enough for him to come. Is something wrong? I can see how you look at him sometimes."

"No, it's just that—oh, never mind. Let's go help Mrs. Ramseyer, shall we?" Beth said, hoping to change the subject.

Sarah nodded. "Sure!"

Beth could see Sarah was uneasy in Benjamin's presence. It did seem to Beth that Benjamin liked Sarah, but the fact remained that he had not acted on it. "Action speaks louder than words," her *vadder* always said.

They hurried over to the waiting buggy and climbed inside. Beth looked over at Sarah and smiled back, happy at least to have her friend along with her for the day. Even though being around Mark usually tended to grate on her nerves, she had a *gut* feeling about that day.

Benjamin looked back at the women before driving off and smiled. "Is everyone ready?"

"We sure are," Sarah said, folding her hands into her lap.

With that, they were off. The cool afternoon air nipped at her as it found its way into the buggy. Beth had no idea where the widow Ramseyer lived, but the tension she felt every time she glanced over at Mark made the trip appear much longer than it really was.

When they finally arrived, Benjamin parked in the yard. He tied his horse to a post while Mark climbed down and headed over toward a large workshop. The women stood together after exiting the buggy, and moments later, Benjamin approached them. "Sarah, you and Beth should go inside and see what needs to be done. Mark and I will start with the firewood," he said, looking out over the property.

"Okay," Sarah said.

The two women headed up the steps to the front door. As they stood there waiting, Beth turned back to see Mark walking into the workshop with his arms already full of wood. Beth did a double take, just as a kindly voice called out from behind her.

"*Gude nochmiddag*! Thank you so much for coming," Rhoda Ramseyer said, her frail hands trembling as she struggled to pull the door open.

"Let me get that," Sarah said, quickly jumping to the woman's aid by holding the door in her stead.

"*Denki*. I've made some lemonade if either of you would like some."

Beth couldn't help but smile at Mrs. Ramseyer's eagerness to do all she could, despite the hardships that had fallen upon her. It reminded Beth of how strong she had always been, but for some reason, she just hadn't been herself since the first day she saw Mark at the Millers' *haus*. Something about how he treated Miriam had awoken some negative emotions deep within her for the first time. Never before had Beth felt so much disdain toward someone. It wasn't acceptable for her to feel that way, and she knew it.

"*Denki* for the offer, but maybe later," Sarah said. "From what Mrs. Miller told us, there's a lot of work for us to help with."

"Unfortunately, that's indeed the case," Mrs. Ramseyer said, slowly making her way into the kitchen. "I just haven't been able to do much lately, especially after my husband passed away."

Beth could see the sadness welling up in Mrs. Ramseyer's eyes, but Sarah must have seen it as well, because she immediately turned to her friend and whispered, "I'm going to sit with her while she has some garden tea. You can start cleaning in the family room if you'd like."

Mrs. Ramseyer was still talking. "I don't know what I would do without that dear boy's help."

Beth was puzzled. "What dear boy?"

"Nash, of course. He's been such a tremendous help to me."

Beth was wondering if she had heard correctly. Sarah must have felt the same way, as she blurted out, "Nash? Nash Grayson?"

Mrs. Ramseyer nodded. "Such a lovely boy. He always fetches the wood in for me. We have lovely long chats."

Sarah and Beth exchanged glances. When Mrs. Ramseyer didn't say anything further, Beth turned to survey the first floor.

"Oh, excuse me!" Mark said, as he passed by closely, nearly brushing against her with the wood he was carrying inside.

Beth stood there, frozen in place, as she watched him work tirelessly to fill the large baskets next to the fireplace. She hadn't even begun cleaning yet, but he was already unloading firewood inside. It made no sense at all why he seemed to be working so diligently. "You might want to be a bit more careful next time," she said, shaking her head.

"I'm so sorry. I was just in a rush and didn't see you there. We're trying to get the wood cut quickly so we can tend to whatever else needs attention or fixing around the property. I'll be more careful next time," he said, flashing a momentary smile that faded right before he headed back outside.

Beth watched him carefully until he was gone, her stomach churning. If he thought he was fooling her, then he was completely wrong. It was all just an act, and she knew it. But what was the purpose? Why was Mark trying so hard to hide his true nature?

After standing still for some time, Beth snapped out of her daze. She gripped the broom in her hand and swept the floors, her mind still focused on Mark and his peculiar behavior. Miriam had told her countless times that Mark was lazy and that he almost walked away from the Amish life during his *rumspringa*. Even after that, she had heard many stories of how he refused to help Miriam's *familye* or any of their neighbors when they were in need. If any of that was true at all, then why did he look like such a hard-working *mann* that day?

Beth was nearly finished with the room when Sarah walked in to check on her. "So, how is everything going in here? I see that the *menner* have brought in a few loads of wood already. *Wunderbar*! That means Mrs. Ramseyer will be all set for some time to come." She then glanced around the room.

"You've done a lovely job in here. Would you like to help me bake now? We're going to make some bread and cookies to last her the week, at least."

"*Jah.*" Beth followed Sarah back to the kitchen.

When they walked in, Mrs. Ramseyer was sitting at the table with a steaming mug before her. "I can't thank you all enough for today. It's been difficult being alone all the time—but not being able to work, as I have all my life, is the most troubling thing," she said, her voice shaky. "Still, I'm no longer lonely, not with Nash to look after me."

Beth and Sarah exchanged glances once more. Was there another Nash Grayson?

At any rate, Mrs. Ramseyer's words affected Beth greatly. Before visiting Mrs. Ramseyer that day, Beth hadn't really put too much thought into how difficult being alone could be. She was already past the normal Amish age for marriage, so it seemed all too likely that she might end up in a similar place—and it terrified her deep down.

"*Denki* again," Mrs. Ramseyer said, sipping happily from her mug.

Beth looked down at the countertop as it sat covered in flour. She glanced over at Sarah, who was kneading the balls of dough vigorously with her hands. As she joined in and began helping, the door swung open.

Mark walked in with a smile on his dirtied face. "We're just about done with the work outside, so Benjamin asked me to see if there was anything else that needs fixing or tending to."

Sarah turned to him and shook her head. "Everything is taken care of in here, and nothing seems broken that would require a *mann's* touch. We're just baking now so that Mrs. Ramseyer will have some food readily available when needed. Then, we'll just have to finish cleaning up and we'll be done as well."

"Okay, I'll let Benjamin know. He's still cutting extra wood and stacking it beside the shed," Mark said. "As I always say, nobody has ever frozen from having too much firewood. Still, there's a mighty big stack of it out there already. Someone else has been cutting it, that's for sure." He turned to head back outside. With his hand on the doorknob, he looked back and added, "Oh, and just so you know, I tidied up the stables and fed the horse. I also cleaned the main buggy, and fixed the old buggy in the yard in case it's needed for travel anytime soon. It looked like one of the wheels was coming undone, but it was a rather easy fix."

"You fixed my husband's buggy?" Mrs. Ramseyer asked, leaning forward in her chair. "I haven't been able to use that since he passed away. It broke the very same day," she added, rubbing at her eyes as her voice grew shakier.

"Well, now you'll be able to use it whenever you need to," Mark said, smiling as he turned and walked outside.

"That was so nice of him," Mrs. Ramseyer said, still a bit teary-eyed. "I hadn't even thought about asking Nash to fix it. It completely slipped my mind, but I'm so happy that Mark cared enough to check it for me."

"That's why we came in the first place," Sarah said. "We're happy to help."

As Beth returned her attention to baking, a range of emotions swarmed over her, causing her to feel a bit numb. Mark was certainly going above and beyond any expectations others could have of him, but why was he putting on such an act? Was he trying to impress someone by hiding who he truly was? Or maybe there was a more selfish excuse for his schemes.

Whatever it might be, Beth was truly beginning to resent him. The better that Mark seemed with each passing day, the more annoyed she grew having to deal with him. If he weren't a liar and a fraud, then he might be the nicest *mann* she had ever met. But he was a fraud; she knew that only too well.

The next person they were to help that day was Elijah Weaver, an elderly man. Mrs. Miller had told Beth that Mr. Weaver was recovering from viral as well as bacterial pneumonia and was staying at his English daughter's house. His English daughter had left the Amish many years ago after her *rumspringa* and had married an English man.

Beth was a little nervous about going to an *Englischer's* house, as she hadn't been in an *Englischer's* house before.

When they arrived, a smiling woman greeted them at the door. "I'm Amy Johnson," she said by way of greeting. "Thanks so much for helping. I have to leave for work for soon. Thank you for visiting with my father. He seems much improved, but he won't be able to go home for a while. Please come in and wait a few moments until the nurse has finished with my father."

Sarah, Mark, Benjamin, and Beth followed Mrs. Johnson inside. As Beth walked in, her attention was taken by a huge mirror running from the floor to the ceiling. She gasped when she caught sight of herself. Beth had often looked at her reflection in store windows, but never had she seen herself full-length in such detail.

Beth turned around when she saw Sarah's reflection appeared next to her. Sarah was also staring at herself. After a moment, Sarah gave a little giggle and pushed Beth forward.

"I never know how long the nurse will take," Mrs. Johnson said, looking at her watch and frowning. "Would you like some tea or coffee? Or maybe a cold drink? I have lemonade."

Sarah said she would like some lemonade, and all the others said they would too. Mrs. Johnson soon returned with glasses of lemonade on a tray and a floral plate filled with peanut butter cookies.

It was all Beth could do not to stare at the room. She recognized the furniture as antique. Mrs. Johnson indicated they should sit on the couch. It was covered with brightly covered cushions and was pale blue in color. *It doesn't look very practical*, Beth thought. *I wonder how she keeps it clean.*

Beth looked over at a sideboard by the window. It was quite a beautiful piece with wooden twists on either side, but it was to the top of it that her atten-

tion was drawn. Tall, deep red glass ornaments sat
on top. They had golden decorations as well as little
roses drawn on them. The droplets appeared to be
made of crystal, but what caught Beth's attention was
that the crystal prism droplets refracted the sunlight
onto the walls, producing shimmering rainbows that
danced along the walls. Beth thought that the *kinner*
would love it.

The rest of the room was overcrowded to Beth's
way of thinking, and she wondered if this was a typical house by English standards. It was well-kept and
clean, but it seemed every spare inch of space was
filled to the brim with furniture and decorations. Two
brass statues of men holding swords stood either side
of the fireplace, and glass ornaments in various colors, along with yellow candles, covered the mantel-
piece. The candles were not lit, but their vanilla aroma
was pungent.

This time, Beth's attention was drawn to a huge
painting. She stared at it until her eyes hurt. It didn't
seem to have any rhyme or reason to it—rather, it
seemed to be a lot of random shapes in bright colors. It didn't appear to be a depiction of anything in
particular.

Under the painting was a deep blue couch of an
unusual shape with a curved back in an arch. This
couch was upholstered in deep blue velvet. Beth figured Mrs. Johnson's favorite color was blue, although
there were other overly bright colors around the room,
particularly on the cushions and on the paintings.

A nurse entered the room and signaled to Mrs.

Johnson that she would like to speak with her in private. The two of them disappeared through a door, but Mrs. Johnson returned only moments later.

"You can see my father now," she said. "I'm late for work. Thank you so much for staying with him."

As they walked into Mr. Weaver's bedroom, Beth saw he was half sitting up in bed. He struggled to raise himself on his pillows.

"All the color has returned to your face. Mr. Weaver," Sarah said. "You look so much better than you did when I saw you the other day."

"I don't feel good, but I do feel better than I did," Mr. Weaver muttered.

Just then, Mrs. Johnson burst through the door. "Dad's cat is up a tree!" she exclaimed. "I'm really late for work and can't be late again this week. I'm sorry to impose, but could somebody please get him down?"

Victor's hand flew to his throat. "My cat," he wheezed. He was clearly distraught.

Mark was the first to speak. "We'll have the cat out of the tree soon. Don't worry, Mrs. Johnson." He hurried out the door after her. Benjamin was hard on his heels. Sarah turned to Mr. Weaver and patted his hand. "Don't you worry about your cat. We'll get him down from the tree."

With that, Beth and Sarah made their way outside. There was a tall tree in the front yard of the house and a scared white cat was clinging to one of the branches. His plaintive meows could be heard clearly.

"Whatever will we do?" Beth said to Sarah.

Benjamin and Mark were looking up the tree. "We'll have to find a ladder," Mark said.

The two men disappeared behind the house. "What if they can't find a ladder?" Beth asked Sarah.

Sarah bit her lip. "They will have to call someone from Mrs. Johnson's phone. Surely everyone has a ladder though."

Beth remained silent. She didn't know if *Englischers* had ladders. After all, this was not a farm. It looked like it had a couple acres, but she could not see any animals grazing. There was an apple orchard to the side, so Beth hoped the Johnsons kept a ladder for the purpose of picking apples. She was relieved when Mark finally returned with an aluminum ladder.

"That's a relief," Sarah said, echoing her thoughts, but Benjamin cut her short.

"It's not long enough," he said. "It's not an extension ladder, but it's not a step ladder."

"It might be fine," Mark said. "I'll go. I'm lighter than you, Benjamin."

Beth looked at the two men. Benjamin was tall and well built, whereas Mark was short and sturdy, not the giant of the man that Benjamin was. Her heart all but stopped. What if the branch broke with Mark? The cat should be all right—she had heard that cats can fall from a height and land safely—but what about Mark?

As Beth watched on in horror, Mark shimmied up the ladder. Of course, that was the easy part. Mark looked down. "Are you holding that ladder tightly, Benjamin?" he asked.

"Sure I am," he said. Beth could see Benjamin had

one leg back for support and was pushing the ladder against the tree with all his strength. It was then she saw with horror that Mark had stepped onto the very top of the ladder with both feet. Beth knew that was not a good idea. For a moment he nearly fell, and everyone gasped, but then he grasped a branch and clung to it.

Benjamin let go of the ladder with one hand and held one of Mark's legs to steady him.

"I'm all right," Mark called down. He somehow managed to swing onto the lower branch, and then climb onto the branch on which the cat was perched.

The cat looked around at Mark and for a moment Beth was afraid the cat would crawl further onto the branch.

"Here kitty, kitty," Mark said in a soothing voice.

Even from her position on the ground, Beth could see that the cat's eyes were wide open with fear. She watched, her heart in her mouth, as Mark edged along the branch a little more.

"Don't go any further, Mark," Benjamin called out. "The branch will break."

Mark was close enough now to reach for the cat. He put one hand around the cat's middle and pulled, but the cat clung on to the tree with all his might. Mark continued to speak in soothing tones to the cat, but his words did not appear to have a calming effect on the cat at all.

Mark still had one hand around the cat, trying to pull the cat from the tree. His other hand was supporting himself on the branch. The cat's body was lifted from the branch, but the cat had a good grip on the tree with his front two paws.

Finally, Mark let go of the branch and seized the cat with both hands. He pulled the cat to him. The cat landed on his chest with an angry yowl.

"Ouch," Mark cried and nearly fell off the branch.

Both Sarah and Beth squealed and clutched each other, but to Beth's great relief, Mark managed to regain his balance. It now seemed the cat was sticking his claws into Mark. Beth could see the pained look on Mark's face as the cat clung to him.

Mark edged his way back along the branch until he reached the tree trunk. That was all well and good, Beth thought, but how on earth would he manage to swing himself back onto the ladder with an angry cat clinging to his chest?

"Be careful," Benjamin called out.

Mark did not respond but gingerly swung his leg back over the branch. To Beth's horror, he teetered on the branch for a moment and then pushed himself back until finally, one foot reached down, seeking the top of the ladder.

Sarah ran over and grabbed his boot and guided it to the top of the ladder. For a while, Beth stood watching in horror. At every moment it looked as though Mark would fall.

After what seemed an age to Beth, Mark's foot was firmly on top of the ladder.

"Take it very slowly now," Benjamin said. "I can't steady you until you're down the ladder a little further."

When Mark's feet reached the lower rungs of the ladder, Beth hurried over to him. "Should I try to take the cat?" Mark nodded to Beth and their eyes locked. The look between that passed between them made Beth's heart flutter. After a pause, Beth reached for the cat.

The cat's claws were digging into him, so she extracted one little paw at a time. As she carefully pried the claws from Mark, she was close enough to smell his manly scent of lime shaving soap, hay, and pine tar shampoo.

Beth soon had the cat in her arms, and thankfully the cat's claws were now retracted. She stroked the cat. "Good kitty, good kitty," she said in a crooning voice. To her relief, the cat purred loudly. She looked up in horror to see little droplets of blood oozing through Mark's shirt.

"Oh Mark, you're hurt!" she said.

"Only some scratches," he said dismissively. "At least the cat is safe."

"You had better put something on that," Beth said with concern.

Mark shook his head. "They're only cat scratches."

"But cat scratches can easily become infected," Sarah said. "Anyway, we had better get this cat to Mr. Weaver or he'll be very upset."

Beth carried the cat carefully into the house. Why did Mark do that? Miriam Hilty said he was a cold, callous man with no feelings for anyone but himself, but yet he had risked his very life for a cat right in front of her eyes.

If Beth had known better, she would have thought Miriam was speaking about another *mann* entirely, because *this* Mark Hostetler seemed kind and caring. Yet she couldn't be mistaken—it had to be one and the same person. So what did Mark possibly think he could gain from rescuing a cat?

She shook her head. It all seemed awfully strange to her.

Mr. Weaver was delighted to see the cat when Beth deposited him into his arms. "Blitz, you naughty cat! You mustn't ever do that again." He broke off and wheezed a little and then added, "Blitz is upset, you see, being away from our house. He hasn't really settled in here."

"Hopefully he'll settle in soon," Mark said.

"*Denki, denki* so much for saving my cat," Mr. Weaver said to everyone.

"It was Mark," everybody said in unison.

Mr. Weaver shot him a wide smile. "*Denki*, Mark."

Beth was startled by Mark touching her shoulder. Electric currents pulsated through her and tingles ran through her body. She sucked in her breath sharply and hoped Mark had not noticed. "*Denki* for getting the cat off me," he said with a smile.

Beth nodded and hurried into the kitchen. She decided to turn her mind to Mr. Weaver's lunch. She was also pondering Mark's motivations for rescuing the cat. *Maybe he really loves animals, yet despises people*, she thought. She had no time to be alone with her thoughts as Sarah came into the kitchen.

"Mr. Weaver said he is not very hungry but would like some caffeine. I mean, he would like *kaffi* soup."

"*Kaffi* soup?" Beth said with a laugh. "I don't know why people like it."

Sarah laughed too. "Mary's very fond of it."

"Does he want it made with saltine crackers or bread?"

"Bread," Sarah said with a chuckle. "He was quite adamant about that. He also wants it made with brown sugar. I know people usually eat it for breakfast, but maybe he didn't have any breakfast this morning."

Beth looked for the bread while Sarah attempted to make the coffee. "How can anybody make coffee with this machine?" she asked Beth.

"I don't have a clue," Beth said with concern. "Is there another way to make coffee here?" They looked through the cupboards and finally concluded that the mysterious electric machine was the only way to make it. They found some coffee pods, but it took quite some experimentation before they figured out how it worked.

Finally, they made some strong milky coffee and poured it over the pieces of bread.

Beth took it into Mr. Weaver. He yawned widely before accepting the bowl. "This is *gut*," he said. "*Denki*. I've lost my appetite, but the nurse said I have to eat a bit."

Beth nodded absently. She was still puzzled by Mark's behavior. He certainly didn't seem to be anything like the *mann* Miriam had described to her.

Chapter Eleven

"Are you up for some fun?" Nash had waited that morning for Jessie Yoder to show up at the ruins of the old, stone cottage.

Jessie narrowed her eyes. "What do you mean?"

Nash shrugged and tried not to look too keen. "I've had an idea how to liven things up around here. When we were at the bishop's *haus* having lunch, it was obvious to me that Sarah Beachy likes Benjamin Shetler. She was jealous that you were flirting with him."

"I was *not* flirting with him!" Jessie sounded indignant, and Nash silently chastised himself for getting her off side.

"Yes, you and I know that," he said in a conciliatory tone, "but Sarah obviously doesn't. She has a huge crush on him."

"So?" Jessie's mouth formed into a pout. "What does that have to do with me?"

"Do you want to help me cause some trouble?"

Jessie looked thoughtful, and Nash's spirits rose. At least she had not rejected his suggestion outright.

"What do you want me to do?"

Nash chewed on a fingernail. "You could flirt with Benjamin a bit in front of Sarah, to annoy her."

Jessie appeared to be thinking it over. "If I agree to do this, how far do want me to go? Should I kiss him?"

Nash didn't like that idea at all. He was very much attracted to Jessie, who was just the sort of girl he liked. Nash was a little hurt that Jessie wanted to kiss Benjamin. What did Benjamin have that he didn't have? He was sure he was just as good looking as Benjamin, and just as tall, and what's more, he wasn't an irritating do-gooder and a boring one at that. Surely Jessie wasn't attracted to a boring man like Benjamin Shetler.

"Well?" Jessie prompted. "Do you want me to kiss him?"

"Sure," Nash said quickly, to hide his true thoughts. It would seem suspicious if he said he didn't want her to, but the truth was, he did not want Jessie Yoder to kiss Benjamin Shetler at all. In fact, the only person he wanted Jessie to kiss was himself. He sighed with frustration.

Jessie took a fruitless swipe at a passing bee.

Nash snorted rudely. "Not very Christian, is it, Jessie? What about 'Thou shalt not kill?' Exodus chapter twenty, verse thirteen."

Jessie was not clearly not amused. "Nash, that's the second time you've been *Scripture Smart*. And of course I wasn't going to hurt the bee. I just didn't want it to land on me. Anyway, I don't like your idea."

Nash pulled a face. "Have I ever asked you to do anything for me before?"

"Yes, as a matter of fact, lots of things."

Nash figured that was quite the exaggeration. He thought it over. Finally, he said, "Do you have anything better to do?"

Jessie was silent for a while. "No. If it's so important to you, I'll do it but just this once. Don't ask me again!"

Jessie Yoder crushed the cigarette under her foot. It was about time she gave them up. She had only taken up the habit to annoy her *mudder*. After her initial satisfaction in succeeding in horrifying her *mudder*, she was now left with a bad habit.

Yet that did not concern Jessie at this moment. What concerned her was that Nash Grayson wanted her to kiss Benjamin Shetler. She had thought that Nash was growing interested in her, but now she realized that it only been because he wanted to use her as a pawn in his game of amusement. How wrong could she have been? She was a fool to have let herself have feelings for Nash. She'd had crushes before, sure, one of them being Jacob Hostetler, but she had been much younger then, and unwise.

She found Nash exciting, with his dangerous looks, his tattoos and piercings, and she found his sneaky ways intriguing. Now, for the first time, Jessie discovered what it was like to be on the receiving end of tricks and plots. She didn't like it at all, not one little bit. In fact, it suddenly brought home to her all the hurt that the tricks she had played on others over the years had caused. She felt truly remorseful for the first time.

Chapter Twelve

Sarah sat on the hard wooden benches in the large reception room at the Flickingers' B&B, as this was where the biweekly church meeting was being held that day. She was wondering why things could never be easy for her. Her *mudder* had died, and then her *vadder* had told her that he was not, in fact, her biological *vadder*, but that her biological *vadder* had died when she was a *boppli*. And as if that was not bad enough, she had run away and had gotten mixed up with the wrong crowd, and had been arrested.

She thought her life had turned around when she had met Martha Miller and then had been welcomed with open arms by the Millers, but then her *vadder* had sent Benjamin Shetler to talk her into returning home—Benjamin, the only *mann* she had ever loved, but who did not love her in return.

Could things get any worse? Sarah turned her attention back to the ministers. The thirty minute initial preaching had ended, and the people now kneeled for the silent prayer. Sarah absently thought that her knee hurt where she had tripped over a rock the other day. She shifted her weight to relieve the niggling pain.

Sarah was relieved when everyone stood for the reading of the chapter from Martin Luther's German Bible. *I must ask Mrs. Miller for some arnica cream for my knee*, she thought, while sneaking a glance at Benjamin. The minister started by reading from the lectionary about the Gospel of Matthew, and then went on to say that we should all submit to the will of *Gott*. The minister also said we should be patient while we wait for the will of *Gott* to unfold.

Sarah sent up a silent prayer that she would be able to submit to the will of *Gott*; after all, she *wanted* to—she would just have to try a little harder.

Finally, the long service was over and Sarah went to the kitchen to help Mrs. Flickinger and the other ladies prepare the food. She was just as quickly shooed back out, and told by the kind ladies to join the other *youngie*.

Sarah made her way over to Martha and Moses, but saw they were joining their *schweschders* and *bruders*, Hannah and Noah, and Esther and Jacob, and their *kinner*. Mary and David were gazing into each other's eyes. Sarah didn't want to intrude, so walked over to sit by herself on a wooden and iron bench under a weeping willow. There was a little garden bed nearby, and Sarah breathed in the sweet scent of the trumpet-shaped honeysuckles, the spicy fragrance of the prolific sweet williams, and the pungent scent of the beautiful, blue hyacinths.

So engrossed was Sarah in looking at the flowers, that she did not hear anyone approach. "Oh, it's you," she said, and then instantly regretted her tone.

Benjamin loomed over her. "May I sit with you?"

"Of course, please do." Sarah made her tone sound inviting.

"Have you given any thought to coming back home?"

Sarah's heart sank. She kept hoping that Benjamin was in love with her, despite all evidence to the contrary. Again, her heart soared when he sat next to her, only to plummet when he asked the question.

"*Nee*," she snapped. "I am not going home, not ever, and that's final."

Benjamin turned his warm gaze upon her, and moved a little closer along the bench to her. "I'm so sorry, Sarah. I didn't mean it to come out like that. I wasn't pressuring you, truly. I just wanted to know if you intend to stay here or go back."

Sarah was bewildered. He wasn't trying to pressure her? But surely that was his only reason for being here?

Benjamin must have suspected what she was thinking, for he continued, "That's not the only reason I came here." He hesitated, and a slow flush traveled up his face. "It was…" he began, before Jessie Yoder rudely and abruptly cut him off.

"*Hiya*, you two," she said. "Can I sit with you?"

Before anyone could answer, Jessie planted herself on the bench between Sarah and Benjamin, and then moved a little closer to Benjamin. She completely ignored Sarah, and turned to Benjamin, asking him how he had liked the church meeting.

It seemed to Sarah that Jessie was flirting outrageously, and giggling quite loudly and often. What's more, Benjamin was making no attempt to get away from Jessie. *I wonder what Benjamin was going to say to me?* Sarah thought. Again, she had gotten her hopes up only to have them dashed. *Just face facts. He doesn't like you*, she scolded herself silently.

Sarah got up and walked away. As she did, she saw the tall, brooding figure of Nash Grayson standing in front of the B&B front porch, staring at Jessie and Benjamin. A chill ran up her spine. *He's up to no good*, she thought.

Nash stared at Jessie flirting with Benjamin. *She's got a nerve, flirting with him like that*, he thought, but then remembered that he had told her to. *Well, she doesn't have to be quite so enthusiastic about it*, he thought with growing irritation. He walked back inside the B&B and slammed the door as hard as he could.

Jessie knew that Nash was watching her. *I hope he's jealous*, she thought, and she flirted with Benjamin all the more. She could see Benjamin was uncomfortable with her behavior, but she didn't care. She figured she was not hurting Benjamin's feelings at all, and if she could use him to make Nash jealous, then she would.

When Nash stormed off and slammed the door of

the B&B, Jessie's spirits rose. *Perhaps he is jealous after all*, she thought with satisfaction. She abruptly left the puzzled Benjamin and walked over to speak to Sarah.

Sarah watched Jessie approach her with some apprehension. She knew Jessie well enough to know that she wasn't going to make small talk.

When Jessie reached Sarah, she came straight to the point. "I have a confession."

"You do?" Sarah was concerned. She did not trust Jessie after the things she'd heard about her, and wondered if this was perhaps part of some game Jessie was playing.

Jessie nodded. "*Jah*. But if I tell you, you can't tell anyone." When Sarah looked at her blankly, she continued, "Agreed?"

"Oh, *jah*. I mean, *nee*. I won't tell anyone." Sarah was somewhat intrigued.

"I've told *Gott* that I won't hurt anyone's feelings anymore," Jessie said, without any trace of embarrassment. "So I have to tell you this. Nash asked me to flirt with Benjamin."

"He did?" Sarah's voice rose to a high pitch, so Jessie took her by the arm and guided, or rather pulled, her down to a row of trees.

"*Shush*. Yes he did, but this puts me in a difficult position as I don't want to betray Nash either." Jessie sighed dramatically. "That's why you can't tell anyone."

"But why?" Sarah was more puzzled than ever.

Jessie shrugged. "Nash is bored, I guess. He can see that you and Benjamin like each other so he wants to cause trouble."

"But we don't, err, he doesn't…" Sarah began, but her curiosity overcame her. "Why would Nash want to cause trouble?"

"How should I know? I'm not a therapist." Jessie's tone grew less tolerant. "Look, I didn't want to tell you, but I don't want to hurt your feelings. You can't tell anyone, okay?"

"Sure."

"All right then, you and Benjamin can go live happily ever after." Jessie looked Sarah up and down, and then walked away, leaving a bewildered Sarah behind.

Could this all be true? It certainly would explain Jessie's recent behavior, and it was something Nash was likely to do, from what Rebecca had told her of the goings on at the B&B.

More importantly, could Jessie be right about Benjamin liking her? It seemed that both Jessie and Nash assumed that Benjamin liked her. Sarah had been over this a thousand times, usually at night when she was trying to sleep. Sometimes she thought Benjamin liked her, but then the normal thing for him to do would be to ask her on a buggy ride, and he had not done that.

More than anything, Sarah wanted to be Benjamin's *fraa*. Just as she was coming to terms with the fact she never would be, her hopes had been raised again. Was this the will of *Gott*, or a cruel trick? Sarah had no idea.

Chapter Thirteen

After the church meeting, the young people filed into the large reception room for their turn for the meal. Church spread, made of marshmallows and peanut butter, was everywhere, as were bowls of a mixture of potato chips, corn chips, popcorn, and crackers, as well as numerous trays of dessert bars and cookies. Jugs of water, and pots of *kaffi*, meadow tea, and cocoa were placed around the table at intervals.

Sarah was still puzzled by Jessie's confession. She wanted to tell Mary and the Miller *schweschders* all about it, but they were all consumed with helping with Hannah's and Esther's *kinner*.

Sarah sat at the table and helped herself to bread and church spread, thinking with a giggle that she was glad the kindly Fannie Graber did not make these sandwiches. Although she was surrounded by other girls, she felt all alone, and left the meal early to have some time to herself outside. Besides, she wasn't particularly hungry.

Sarah walked back to the bench under the weeping willow again, hoping Benjamin would seek her out, while at the same time telling herself that such thoughts were foolish.

This time, it was not Benjamin who approached her, but Nash Grayson. Nash made no attempt to sit next to her, but stood in front of her, towering over her, his arms folded, and the corners of his lips turned up. "Why are you sitting out here all alone?" he asked with narrowed eyes.

"I wanted time to myself," Sarah said, hoping that would not sound rude.

Nash laughed. "I can take a hint. Anyway, I thought you'd be over with your cousins." He gestured to where the Miller *schweschders* were playing with the *kinner* at the far end of the garden.

"They're not my cousins," Sarah said. "They're *gut* friends, but not relatives."

Nash put his hand to his mouth in a manner which looked to Sarah to be entirely fake, and at the same time, made the hair on the back of her neck stand up. "Oh, I'm sorry, you don't know."

"Know what?" Sarah asked with growing apprehension. She could feel a hard knot form in the pit of her stomach.

"They *are* your cousins. I'm sorry, I had no idea you didn't know," Nash said coyly. "Benjamin didn't tell me that you didn't know. He didn't say it was a big secret or anything."

Sarah momentarily put her hands to her head. The world spun. She grasped the hard edge of the seat with both hands and tried to fight the growing nausea. "I don't know what you mean," she managed to say.

"Sorry. Forget I said anything." Nash turned and made to leave.

Sarah stood up. "Nash! Wait, what's going on? You have to tell me."

Nash turned around, and Sarah saw the calculating glint in his eye. "Your father, well, your *step*father Samuel Beachy, was from my parents' community. Didn't you know?"

Sarah shook her head. The confusion was giving her a throbbing headache, and she was worried she'd be physically sick.

"Well, I shouldn't be the one to tell you," Nash continued, unable to keep the smugness out of his voice, "but your father was Mr. Miller's brother."

Sarah gasped.

"Isn't that a coincidence," Nash continued, his voice seeming to Sarah to come from far away, "and the Miller family and Benjamin didn't even bother to tell you. I wonder why?"

Sarah pushed past Nash and ran away, the muted sound of Nash's cruel laughter following her. She ran blindly down past the B&B, down past the ruins of the old stone cottage, until she lost her footing and fell heavily, landing on her sore knee. Sarah picked herself up, and burst into tears.

At once, a strong hand grasped her arm and she

was helped gently to her feet. She looked up into the concerned eyes of Benjamin.

"Are you hurt?"

Sarah shook her head and dusted the dirt from her apron.

"You're trembling."

Sarah shook her head again and hurriedly wiped the tears from her eyes.

The next thing she knew, she was pulled against Benjamin's hard chest and he was stroking her hair. She reveled in his manly scent and strong arms. She wanted to stay there forever, safe and warm.

Yet Nash's words rang loudly through her ears: *Benjamin didn't tell me you didn't know*, and, *Benjamin didn't even bother to tell you*.

She pushed Benjamin away and clapped her hands over her ears, as if that would make the thoughts stop.

"Why did you tell Nash and not tell me?" she snapped.

Benjamin frowned, clearly puzzled by Sarah's accusatory words and her abrupt change in attitude. "Tell Nash what?" he asked, scratching his head.

"How could you, Benjamin? I thought I could trust you! How could you do this to me?" Sarah ran from Benjamin, leaving him staring after her in bewilderment.

Sarah reached the Miller *familye* buggy just as Mr. and Mrs. Miller were about to leave.

"Don't you want to stay with the *youngie* for the afternoon?" Mrs. Miller asked, clearly concerned about Sarah's red, puffy eyes.

Sarah shook her head. "*Nee*, I just want to get home, and then there is something important I want to ask you."

"Whatever has happened, child?"

Sarah dabbed at her eyes and said, "Please, can it wait until we are back in the *haus*?"

Mrs. Miller nodded and the short journey was spent in tense silence. When they arrived at the *haus*, Mr. Miller promptly made himself scarce, while Mrs. Miller and Sarah went into the *haus*.

The soft, puffy clouds and the blue sky were being replaced by rolling, threatening clouds, and the sun was already behind billowing, black clouds. *Just like my mood*, Sarah thought.

Mrs. Miller made herself and Sarah some hot meadow tea, and then sat at the kitchen table, her face white and drawn. "What is this about, Sarah?" she asked in a kindly tone.

Sarah wondered where to begin, but then thought she might as well blurt it all out. She took a deep breath, and then launched into her explanation. "Nash Grayson told me that Mr. Miller's *bruder* was my real *vadder*."

At this, Mrs. Miller gasped and her hand flew to her mouth. Sarah was concerned that Mrs. Miller might faint, and forgot her own problems for the moment. "Mrs. Miller, are you okay?"

Mrs. Miller clutched at her throat and waved her on. "Tell me what he said," she said in a hoarse voice.

"Nash said that Mr. Miller's *bruder* was my biological father, and that my *daed*, well that is, Samuel

Beachy, the *mann* I thought was my *daed*, was from Nash's community. That's all. Isn't that bad enough?" she added defiantly.

The color was returning to Mrs. Miller's cheeks somewhat although she was wringing her hands restlessly. "You deserve a full explanation," she said.

Sarah sat in silence, waiting for Mrs. Miller to continue. "My husband Abraham's *bruder*, Shem, was your *vadder*," she said. "He married your *mudder*, Mary Lengacher, and they had you. Abraham and Shem were close, but your *mudder* never really got on with any of us. Shem died when you were still a little *boppli*. Your *mudder* was from southern Indiana."

Sarah knew where her *mudder* was from, and could contain herself no longer. "Why wasn't I told?"

"I'm getting to that," Mrs. Miller said patiently. "Like I said, our *familye* did not get on well with your *mudder*, Mary Lengacher. We saw her at Shem's funeral of course, but then did not see her again until you were six months old. She brought you here and said she was getting remarried. We were surprised of course, so soon after your *vadder* had died. It was not our place to judge," Mrs. Miller added primly, the corners of her mouth turning down.

Sarah waited with bated breath to hear what else Mrs. Miller had to say.

Mrs. Miller cleared her throat, took a sip of meadow tea, and then pressed on. "Your *mudder* told us that you were too young to remember your *vadder*, so she was going to raise you as her new husband's *dochder*. Abraham and I at first did not realize what

she meant, but she made us promise that we would
not tell you. When we realized that she had no intention of telling you that your *vadder* was, in fact, Shem
Miller, we had a falling out, and that was the last we
ever saw of you. We knew that they had changed your
name to your new *vadder's*, to Beachy and not Miller,
as would be expected, and we heard that they had no
children of their own, but that was all."

A loud clap of thunder made both women jump.
Mrs. Miller hurried over to shut the kitchen window
before the first drops of rain fell.

Sarah was hard put to process all this information
at once. "Why didn't you tell me any of this when I
arrived here?" she asked.

The color drained from Mrs. Miller's face once
again. "It wasn't our place. Abraham and I discussed
it, but we considered that it was your *vadder's* place
to tell you. As he hadn't told you, we felt it wasn't the
right thing to do for us to tell you. We felt *Gott* had
blessed us by sending you to us after all these years,"
she added with emotion in her voice.

"So, did you ever meet my *vadder*, err, Samuel
Beachy?"

Mrs. Miller shook her head, just as another clap of
thunder sounded. "*Nee*. Your *mudder* made it clear
that we were not invited to the wedding."

Sarah sipped her tea and thought things over. Her
mudder had been a very strict woman. Her *vadder*
was strict, but her *mudder* more so. Perhaps her *vadder* had not told her the truth out of respect for his
fraa's wishes. Samuel Beachy may not have been her

biological *vadder*, but he was the only *vadder* she had ever known.

Sarah was upset that so many people had lied to her, by keeping the information about her birthright from her. Sure, she could see why Mr. and Mrs. Miller had done so, in order to respect her *mudder's* wishes, but what was Benjamin's excuse? She looked up to see Mrs. Miller regarding her carefully.

"Are you all right, Sarah?"

"*Jah*, but it's a lot to take in. It's a terrible shock." Her voice was quiet.

"*Jah, jah*." Mrs. Miller nodded with a sympathetic expression on her face. "I'm so sorry we kept the information from you, but we felt we had no choice, since your *vadder* himself hadn't told you."

Sarah nodded. "But why didn't Benjamin tell me?"

"Benjamin?" Mrs. Miller's face went blank.

"*Jah*, Benjamin Shetler. Nash said that it was Benjamin who told him that my *vadder* was Mr. Miller's *bruder*."

Mrs. Miller's face turned as black as the clouds outside. "*Phsaw*," she hissed. "That no-gooder! Do not listen to likes of Nash Grayson, child. He would not know the truth if it fell upon him from the skies above. I fancy he said that simply to cause trouble between you and Benjamin, who is a *gut mann*, by all reports. Unlike that Nash," she added with annoyance.

Sarah just wanted to crawl into a hollow log and let the world go by. This was all too much for her. She had just found out she was a Miller, which she considered to be a *gut* thing, but what was not so *gut* was that her *vadder* and *mudder* had kept this from her all her life, and she had found out only by accident. And what was more, she had made a fool of herself with Benjamin and wrongfully accused him of lying. Would he ever forgive her?

Sarah went to her room and paced up and down the small area for what seemed to her like hours, and was unable to eat for the rest of the day. Her stomach was churning and her heart was racing. Never had she been so tense.

Chapter Fourteen

Nash and Jessie were once more down by the ruins of the old stone cottage, where they now met most mornings, while Jessie smoked a cigarette.

Jessie had, in fact, given up smoking several days earlier, but Nash had not noticed. *Too self-absorbed*, Jessie figured.

Today Nash was complaining once again about his parents. "They've given me the worst room at the B&B," he complained.

"Well, it's free, isn't it?" Jessie snapped.

Nash was used to Jessie's forthright manner and was not offended. "Yes, but I'm their son, so they should look after me."

Jessie shrugged. "Whatever. Well, you should at least clean up your own room."

Nash folded his arms. "Why should I? That's what they pay *you* to do."

Jessie rolled her eyes. "They pay me to clean

rooms for *guests*," she said. "You're not a guest, you're a freeloader."

Nash laughed. He enjoyed their banter, even if he was on the receiving end of insults, as usual. He found all other girls boring, but Jessie was far from boring, and what's more, she kept him on her toes. "I'm getting a job," he announced out of the blue.

Jessie's mouth dropped open. "What, you? A job? Doing what?"

"Construction, gazebos mainly," Nash said smugly. "I'm going to work for Amos Troyer."

"Has he met you?" Jessie asked, her face clearly showing her disbelief.

Nash snorted rudely. "What kind of question is that? Yes, of course. I went for the interview and he offered me the job. I want a steady job with a steady income."

Jessie snickered rudely. "You?"

Nash narrowed his eyes at her. "Yes, me. Why are you so surprised?"

Jessie laughed outright. "I thought your only income was betting on the horses. Besides, you seem the lazy type to me."

"Well, I'm not," Nash snapped, disappointed the way the conversation was going, and a little hurt by Jessie's attitude. "And I haven't gambled for ages. I owe money and I have to pay it back, since my parents couldn't be bothered to pay it for me."

"Why should they?"

"What? Well, I'm their son."

Jessie walked over to stand in front of Nash and

jabbed her finger into his chest. "Where do you get this sense of entitlement from? You're acting like a spoiled brat. You're not ten years old! Do you expect them to still look after you when you're thirty or even fifty?"

Nash opened his mouth to say something, but Jessie continued. "And what would *Gott* think of that? But I suppose you turned your back on *Gott* when you went on *rumspringa*."

Nash was highly offended. "I did not!" he said. "That's a stupid thing to say. People don't leave God when they go on *rumspringa*, even if they're on a long one."

Jessie merely shrugged, and turned to look over the fields. "Are you ever going to return to the community?"

Nash walked over to stand beside her. "Dunno. It depends."

Jessie looked up at him. "On what?"

Nash pulled a face and shrugged one shoulder. *On whether you'll be my girlfriend*, he thought. Thinking of Jessie as his girlfriend brought up thoughts of jealousy over Benjamin, so he asked, "How was the Singing last night?"

"It was okay, I suppose." Jessie walked a few steps away from Nash.

Nash followed her and stood in front of her again. "Was Benjamin there?"

"*Jah*."

"Did you flirt with him?" Nash held his breath, anxiously awaiting her answer.

Jessie crushed a small stone under her boot. "I'm not playing that game anymore."

Nash frowned. What did Jessie mean? Did it mean she was truly attracted to Benjamin so would not play games with him? Or was she simply tired of pretending to like Benjamin in order to upset Sarah?

Before Nash could ask, Jessie continued, "Besides, Sarah wasn't even there."

Nash hit himself on the side of the head. "Oh, of course, I forgot to tell you." He chuckled, and then added, "What until you hear what I did."

Jessie looked at him expectantly. *She'll love this*, Nash thought. Aloud he said, "I overheard my parents say they thought that Sarah's stepfather was Samuel Beachy, and that he left our community years ago to marry a widow with a *boppli*. Anyway, I called a friend of mine who's on *rumspringa*. His mother knows everything about everyone in our community. He called me back the night before last to tell me— wait 'til you hear this—that Sarah's father was, in fact, Mr. Miller's brother!"

Jessie's raised her eyebrows. "Are you saying that Sarah's *vadder* was Mr. Miller's *bruder*?"

Nash nodded with delight. "Yes, and he died, and so Sarah's mother married Samuel Beachy soon after. But this is the main thing, Sarah didn't know."

"She didn't know what?"

Nash sighed. "Pay attention. Sarah didn't know that Mr. Miller's brother was her biological father. Her parents never told her, and the Millers didn't either."

Jessie chewed her lip. "I wonder why no one told her?"

Nash was a little let down that Jessie didn't seem too surprised. "Who cares? Anyway, she knows now, because I told her yesterday, and she was so upset." Nash burst into laughter, but was puzzled when Jessie's face flushed red.

"I'm not sure I understand," she said slowly. "Are you telling me that Sarah Beachy's biological father was Mr. Miller's *bruder*, but that Sarah had no idea?"

Nash nodded, pleased with himself.

"And you told Sarah all this yesterday?"

Nash nodded again, and then laughed. "If only you could've seen her face." He laughed some more.

"Why, that's so mean!" Jessie yelled, causing Nash to take a step back. "I knew you were selfish and self-absorbed, but I didn't know you were cruel too!"

Nash was taken aback. He was puzzled by Jessie's reaction. "Well, that's rich coming from you," he snapped.

"What do you mean?" Jessie said each word slowly.

Nash should have been warned by her tone, but he was not. "I hadn't been here long before I heard all about you." Nash pointed to Jessie for emphasis. "Everyone talks about how you tried to break up Esther and Jacob."

An offended look passed over Jessie's face. "I was young and silly, and thought I was in love with him," she said.

"That's no excuse."

Jessie stamped her foot. "I was *not* defending my

actions to *you*," she yelled. "It's obvious in hindsight I was mean, but I went to the bishop over it. Not that it's any of your business. You're cruel, you're shallow, and you're mean."

With that, Jessie stormed off.

Women! Nash thought, staring after Jessie's rapidly disappearing back. *There's no understanding them. I bet all those cigarettes she smokes are making her angry for no good reason. She'll come to her senses sooner or later.*

Chapter Fifteen

Mrs. Miller had invited over her four *dochders*, Hannah, Esther, and Martha, along with their husbands who also happened to be *bruders*, Noah, Jacob, and Moses, of course, their *kinner*. Hannah's twins were looking for Sarah's big, ginger cat, Tom, but he had the good sense to stay out of their way and had made himself scarce for the evening.

Hannah, Esther, and Martha were all expecting, and were teasing Rebecca that it would be her turn next. "Stop teasing me," Rebecca insisted, "It's not fair. It's just like when you all teased me because I would be the last Miller *maidel* to get married."

"But we didn't know at the time that you *weren't* going to be the last Miller girl to be married," Esther said. "There's one more to go after you marry Elijah: Sarah."

Everyone turned to smile at Sarah. Sarah had felt somewhat overwhelmed that the Miller *schweschders* had been delighted when they found out she was their cousin. Mrs. Miller was having this dinner in honor of that fact, and Sarah was a little uneasy at being the center of attention.

"So you don't have morning sickness this time?" Sarah asked Esther, in an attempt to divert their attention away from herself. "Martha told me you had it badly with Isabel."

"*Nee*, not this time," Esther said, and then laughed. "Thank goodness. None at all this time. I think I had it bad enough with Isabel to make up for several *bopplin*."

"Then perhaps you are having a boy this time," Mrs. Miller said.

Esther looked puzzled, but made no attempt to disagree with her *mudder*. Although Mrs. Miller had suffered morning sickness with her four girls, Hannah had no morning sickness when she was having her twins, one boy and one girl.

"I was worried when I saw how sick Esther was when she was expecting with Isabel," Martha said, "but I've been fine too."

Sarah bounced Esther's *boppli*, Isabel, on her knee, thinking how lovely it would be to have her own *bopplin* and have her own husband, preferably Benjamin Shetler. Perhaps their *bopplin* would have sandy colored hair, all messy like Benjamin's, and have his big brown eyes. They would have several *kinner*, all of whom would grow up tall like their *vadder*, and be tender and compassionate and lovable.

"Are you all right, Sarah?" Mrs. Miller said. "Your

eyes have gone somewhat glazed. You don't feel sick again, do you?"

"Oh, I was just daydreaming." Sarah was embarrassed to be caught out. She hoped Mrs. Miller wouldn't ask her what she had been daydreaming about.

"Will *Datt* be in soon?" Hannah asked her *mudder*, and Sarah shot Hannah a grateful look.

"I hope so," Mrs. Miller said. "He said he'd be in as soon as he finishes showing Benjamin around the workshop."

"Benjamin?" Sarah shrieked and then everyone turned to look at her.

"Oh, didn't I mention that Benjamin is coming to dinner too?" Mrs. Miller's eyes opened wide in innocence, and then she hurried into the kitchen.

"I told you *Mamm* was a very keen matchmaker," Martha said, and her three *schweschders* nodded.

"There's just no stopping her," Hannah said, "I could tell you stories. In fact, I think I already have." She chuckled.

"You might as well marry him now. There's no fighting *Mamm*," Rebecca added.

"Mrs. Miller wants me and Benjamin to marry?" Sarah asked in a small voice.

The four *schweschders* nodded.

Sarah chewed the edge of her thumb. "But I don't think he likes me."

"*Mamm* won't let a little thing like that get in the way," Rebecca said, but was soon hushed by her three *schweschders*.

"Of course he likes you," Martha said. "I've seen the way he looks at you."

"But we had a fight. I accused him of telling Nash that I was, well, that I was your cousin."

"Did he?" Rebecca asked.

"I don't know, but I doubt it." Sarah absently rubbed her forehead.

"It's nothing that can't be sorted out," Martha said, but they all stopped speaking as soon as Mrs. Miller returned.

Mrs. Miller deposited a large pot of vegetable soup on the table. "That's right, stop speaking as soon as I come in the room. I know nothing, I'm just a silly old woman." Mrs. Miller stormed out of the room and presently the sound of pots and pans banging emanated from the kitchen.

The *schweschders* chuckled softly. Martha opened her mouth to say something, but Mr. Miller came through the door, followed by Benjamin.

Sarah didn't know where to look. She stole a glance at Benjamin and noted that he didn't look his usual, confident self.

Mrs. Miller emerged from the kitchen. "Rebecca and Martha, both of you come and help me with the *schnitz und knepp*," she ordered. "Mary is out with David." Sarah stood up to help too, but Mrs. Miller fixed her with a steely gaze. "You stay there, Sarah, and talk to our guest."

Sarah was embarrassed by Mrs. Miller's overt matchmaking attempts, and saw that the Miller *schweschders* were all exchanging amused glances.

Mr. Miller went over to talk to his sons-in-law, the Hostetler *bruders*, in the other room, while Benjamin sat opposite Sarah.

"*Hiya*, Sarah."

"*Hiya*, Benjamin," Sarah said shyly.

"Err, congratulations," Benjamin said.

Sarah was puzzled. "Congratulations for what?"

"Err, for being a Miller," Benjamin said, and then his face turned beet red.

Sarah's heart went out to him. Clearly he was nervous and didn't know what to say. "*Denki*," she said brightly.

Mrs. Miller summoned everyone to the table. Along with the vegetable soup, she, Martha, and Rebecca had deposited plates piled high with *schnitz und knepp*, and the mouth-watering scent of smoked ham, apples, and brown sugar wafted through the room.

The large, rectangular table was big enough to seat the adults, and the *kinner* sat obediently nearby at a little table that Mr. Miller had newly built for them. Mrs. Miller seated Sarah opposite Benjamin.

Sarah fidgeted, as a range of conflicting emotions ran through her. She was in love with Benjamin. She had been for years. The question on her mind now, and the question which had raised its head many a time in the middle of a sleepless night, was whether he shared her feelings? Sarah had never known him to take any other girl on a buggy ride, and he had held her close when she was upset over Nash's revelation. Yet was he only being kind? It was not the done thing for a young *mann* to hold a girl like that, so Sarah figured, or rather hoped, that it meant he did have feelings for her.

And even if he did have feelings for her, had those feelings dissipated after she had wrongfully accused him of telling Nash about her biological father?

Sarah shook her head, but then looked up and saw Benjamin looking at her with his big, brown eyes. *He has eyes just like a puppy*, she thought wistfully. Sarah held Benjamin's gaze for a moment, and then looked away. Something had passed between them, of that she was sure. Her stomach fluttered and her heart raced.

Sarah had made up her mind. No matter how embarrassing it might prove to be, she would apologize to Benjamin at the first opportunity. Sarah knew at that point what her father's expression, "He wished the floor would open up and swallow him," really meant. Her cheeks grew hotter and hotter. She had known this night would not turn out well.

There was happy chatter over the meal, but that stopped as soon as Mr. Miller spoke to Benjamin. "Well, Benjamin, it's all handcrafted of course."

"What is?" Mrs. Miller looked perplexed, and waved a spoon in the direction of her husband.

"Why, the furniture, obviously."

Mrs. Miller muttered to herself.

Undaunted, Mr. Miller pushed on. "We do the finish by hand. We do custom pieces, as well as the pieces we sell in our store. It's all made here though."

Mrs. Miller stood up and cleared the plates. "I

haven't finished yet," Mr. Miller said plaintively, but Mrs. Miller removed his plate nonetheless.

Rebecca and Martha went into the kitchen to help Mrs. Miller with dessert. Sarah wondered whether she should accompany them, but decided not to, after Mrs. Miller had refused her offer of help earlier. After all, she didn't want to make Mrs. Miller angry. She was already angry enough, judging by the sound of the pots and pans.

Benjamin appeared engrossed by Mr. Miller's discussion of the fine points of furniture making, and Sarah wondered whether it was genuine interest or whether Benjamin was simply being polite.

Mrs. Miller came back out of the kitchen. "We're having chocolate peppermint whoopie pies," she announced, "but I forgot to gather the peppermint for the top. Sarah, would you and Benjamin mind gathering some peppermint for me please?"

"It doesn't take two of them, surely," Mr. Miller protested, before he caught his *fraa's* withering glare.

"And, Abraham, give them a lamp to take with them."

"They won't be out there long enough for a lamp. It's only just getting dark now," Mr. Miller said, clearly not realizing what his *fraa* was up to. Sarah, however, was only too painfully aware, and the others were all doing their best to hide their amusement.

"It gets dark quickly," Mrs. Miller snapped, before turning on her heel and storming back into the kitchen.

Sarah's cheeks were warm with embarrassment.

She dutifully took the lamp from Mr. Miller and walked outside with Benjamin.

Sarah wondered how long she could continue to give her heart to Benjamin without some sign that he loved her back. As she looked at him now, standing in the dusk, the twilight casting playful shadows around his face, Sarah felt the weight of heartache brought on by years of loving someone with no response.

Sarah looked at the little weeds poking their heads through the gravel. *It reflects the state of my heart*, she thought with great sadness.

Sarah waited for Benjamin to open the little gate to the herb and vegetable garden, and then walked through, before turning to Benjamin. She expelled a long breath before speaking. "Benjamin, I'm sorry I believed Nash over you. Actually, it was all such a shock, I wasn't thinking straight. Will you forgive me?"

Benjamin's face lit up. "Of course I forgive you. There's nothing to forgive."

Sarah, delighted by Benjamin's words, was not paying attention to what she was doing as she bent to pluck some peppermint leaves, still smiling to herself.

At that moment, Sarah's boot went out from under her and she threw out her hands to stay her fall. Benjamin caught her and held her close to him. She could feel his warm breath on her cheek. Instinctively she lifted her gaze and was suddenly staring into the depths of brown that were Benjamin's eyes. She couldn't move her eyes from his; it was as if they were locked together, frozen in a moment of time—a moment that Sarah wanted to treasure forever. In his gaze there was no time; there was no tomorrow and no yesterday; there was a promise, of that she was sure. Something had passed between them and she was positive that he must have felt it too. It seemed like forever before he released her.

"Ouch!" she exclaimed, realizing her hand had closed hard around a plant. "I think that was nettle!"

Benjamin looked up and met her eye for the briefest of moments, and then studied his boots again. For a moment he did not speak, and then he said, "Not nettle, surely? What would nettle be doing in a herb garden?"

"Mrs. Miller grows nettle for rinsing hair, as well as for nettle tea."

"Oh yes, of course, nettle tea." Benjamin held up the lamp to inspect her hand. "Show me, where does it hurt?"

"This finger mainly."

Benjamin held the finger to his mouth and gently kissed it.

Sarah stood there with her mouth hanging open. *He truly does like me after all*, she thought, still somewhat shocked. Sarah soon revised her opinion, or at least had cause to doubt it, when Benjamin pulled away suddenly, dropping her finger like a hot potato.

"You should go back to the *haus* and put something on that," he said.

"Oh, it's just a little sting," Sarah said, embarrassed by what had just happened. "I'll put some burdock on it. That always works." Sarah took the lamp from Benjamin and looked around for the broad leaves that identified the burdock plant. It was just on dusk, but was the time of day when shapes become blurred. Finding a burdock plant, she plucked a leaf, crushed it between her fingers, and rubbed it into her hand. The stinging eased almost at once.

"Let's go back to the *haus*," Benjamin said again.

Sarah did not understand. Why had Benjamin pulled away suddenly? Was he ashamed he had kissed her hand? He was certainly acting like it.

The two returned to the *haus*. "Where is the peppermint?" Mrs. Miller demanded.

"We didn't get it." Sarah's face burned hot.

Everyone stopped talking and turned to look at them, and Sarah was mortified as to what they must all be thinking. "I hurt my hand on some nettle," Sarah said, "and then I put some burdock on it. With all that, we forgot all about the peppermint."

"I'll go get it now." Benjamin hurried outside.

When Benjamin returned with the mint, the meal progressed happily, yet although there was the happy conversation over dessert, Sarah and Benjamin remained silent.

"Sarah, would you help me in the kitchen? The two of us can manage; the rest of you all stay out here and talk." Martha's tone was firm, and even her *mudder* and *schweschders* did not rise to help.

Sarah and Martha cleared the plates. When they were alone in the kitchen, Martha pulled out a wooden chair and said to Sarah, "Sit down. We have to talk. What happened between you and Benjamin?" Martha and Sarah had become *gut* friends some time ago, after meeting when both were on *rumspringa*, but Sarah hadn't seen much of Martha after she married Moses. Still, their friendship had remained strong.

Sarah put her head in her hands. "Oh it was so awful! It was so embarrassing."

Martha sat down next to Sarah. "What happened?"

"You know how you keep telling me that Benjamin really does like me?"

Martha smiled. "*Jah*, but I've never managed to convince you."

Sarah nodded. "Well, I thought you were right tonight, but then I changed my mind again."

Martha appeared to be growing impatient. "Sarah, please just tell me what happened."

"When we went to gather peppermint, I accidentally put my hand around some nettle."

"Ouch."

Sarah nodded. "For sure. Anyway, Benjamin kissed my hand."

"He what?" Martha all but smirked, and then put her hand over her mouth. "Sorry, go on! Benjamin actually kissed your hand? What happened next?"

"He kissed my hand, but then he suddenly dropped it and acted a bit odd, and then said we should go back to the *haus*."

Martha smiled triumphantly. "He really likes you," she said. "That's proof."

Sarah was puzzled. "What, it's proof that he likes me? I thought it was proof that he *doesn't* like me. I don't understand."

"An Amish *mann* doesn't kiss a girl's hand if he doesn't like her, silly." Martha rolled her eyes.

"But why did he suddenly drop my hand?"

Martha sighed loudly, "Because he likes you. Oh Sarah, really, you have no idea about *menner*."

Sarah had to admit that Martha was right about her having no idea about *menner*. But was Martha right about Benjamin? Did he really like her? And if he did, why hadn't he asked her on a buggy ride yet? She did not have the answers.

Chapter Sixteen

Nash was waiting for Jessie by their usual place, down by the ruins of the old stone cottage. She had not been there the last two mornings in a row; he hoped it would be third time lucky.

When Jessie did appear, a faint wave of nausea washed over Nash. Jessie affected him like no other woman ever had. He had missed her dreadfully the last few days, and he realized that she had done her best to avoid him. He wondered if it was too late for them. Had he already pushed her away before he even had a chance?

Nash stood and looked over the rolling fields. He was beginning to appreciate the countryside and the more relaxed lifestyle and now was not missing the city so much. Yet there was no rest from the questions that kept assaulting his mind. Had Jessie been right? Did he have a sense of entitlement? Was he really a spoiled brat? He had been aware that his mother had often cried about him, and that had made him feel bad, but now the first real pangs of remorse were filtering through to him.

Nash turned around and saw Jessie approaching. She wasn't smiling at him, but then, she wasn't a smiling sort of person. *She's here, and that must be a good sign*, he thought.

"I didn't know if you'd come," he said by way of greeting.

"I didn't know if I would either," said Jessie with her characteristic frankness.

"Why did you then?" Nash realized that his voice had sounded sulky; he hadn't meant it to be.

Jessie shrugged and pouted. "Dunno."

Nash stood, looking at his feet, and moving from one foot to another. After an uncomfortable silence, he decided to speak. *It's now or never*, he thought. "Jessie, would you have dinner with me?"

Jessie appeared to be quite taken aback. "What, like on a date?" Her voice rose to a high pitch.

"Yes, I suppose so."

"You said dinner?"

Nash crossed his arms. "Have you gone deaf?"

When Jessie glared at him, he hurried to continue. "Well, I can't ask you on a buggy ride, can I, seeing that I don't have one. Unless we took your buggy, I suppose."

Jessie shook her head. "*Nee*, we can't take *my* buggy. That wouldn't be right."

Nash was at first irritated, but then he realized Jessie had not rejected him outright. "Well, how about it?"

Jessie narrowed her eyes. "That's not the nicest invitation to a date I've ever had."

Nash laughed. "How many invitations to dates have you had?"

Jessie shrugged. "None."

Nash was nervous, and Jessie's behavior was not helping. She was just standing there looking at him through narrowed eyes, and as yet had not accepted or rejected his invitation. His stomach was churning and all tied up in knots.

Jessie was standing directly in front of him, and her proximity was adding to his nervousness. She smelled heavenly, like vanilla and roses. He gave it one more shot. "Jessie Yoder, would you do me the honor of accompanying me to dinner?" he said with a flourish and a bow.

Jessie laughed. "Okay, why not?"

Nash's heart leaped, and without thinking, he pulled Jessie to him and planted a kiss on her warm lips.

At first Jessie did not resist, but then she pulled away and slapped Nash across the face.

Nash rubbed his smarting cheek. "Aww! What did you do that for?"

"I'm not an English girl. You can't just kiss me."

Is she kidding? Nash thought. "You kissed me back," he pointed out.

"Did not!"

Nash was on the point of saying *Did too*, when he realized how childish that would sound. Why didn't

Jessie let him kiss her? Perhaps she liked Benjamin after all. She had seemed quite keen to kiss him.

"You like Benjamin, don't you?" Nash meant it as a simple question, but it came out as an accusation. Until his words were out, Nash had not admitted to himself just how jealous he had been of Benjamin, just how deep his feelings were for Jessie. From out of nowhere, the Scripture from Matthew 12:34 popped into his mind: *For out of the abundance of the heart the mouth speaketh*. Nash hadn't realized until now that the Scripture meant that people would speak out what really came from deep inside them.

Jessie simply snorted rudely. "Typical! So typical of a *mann* to think that if a girl won't kiss him, it must be because there is someone else."

"Well, is there?"

Jessie rolled her eyes, and stormed off.

Nash was confused by Jessie. One thing he was not confused about was that he had made the decision to return to the community. He supposed there were good and bad people amongst the Amish just as there were good and bad people amongst the English. He would just be one of the not so good people amongst the Amish. *We can't all be goody two shoes like that Benjamin Shetler*, he thought.

Chapter Seventeen

Nash was nervous when Bishop William Graber opened the door to let him inside, despite the fact that the bishop looked like an *Englischer's* idea of Santa Claus, with his long gray beard, round face with red cheeks, and large blue eyes.

Mrs. Graber hurried over to welcome Nash. "*Hiya*, Nash. You look hungry as always. I've made some special sandwiches for you, cucumber and peanut butter, raw liver and nettle, and bacon with chocolate cream. I must get back to my baking. Don't worry, I won't be able to overhear a word you say, so you can speak in complete confidence."

The bishop appeared to be amused. "My *fraa* tells me you enjoy her cooking."

"Yes I do," Nash said, truthfully. *I wouldn't pay for it, but it's free*, he added silently.

"Perhaps we should take the sandwiches out to the porch."

Nash was relieved that the bishop said that. No

matter what Mrs. Graber had said, he was sure she would be able to hear from the kitchen, and he didn't want what he had to say spread all over town. He had no idea whether or not Mrs. Graber would gossip, but he didn't want to take the chance.

Light rain was starting to fall. Nash watched it for a moment and then was glad he had a car and wouldn't be driving home in the rain in a buggy. *Not for long, I'll have to get rid of the car*, he told himself.

"How are your parents doing?" the bishop asked, once they had settled into stiff, old wooden chairs with a round, wooden table between them.

"Good, thank you."

Nash was quite nervous about speaking to the bishop. He didn't know how truthful he should be.

"Let us pray first, and then you can tell me why you have come to see me today. We can eat as we talk," the bishop said.

They both bowed their heads for a silent prayer. For some inexplicable reason, Nash's right eye started to twitch, so he rubbed it hard. Then an uncontrollable urge to laugh came over him, and he had to fight it. *I suppose it's because I'm so nervous*, he thought.

"Now, Nash, have a sandwich and tell me why you came to see me today."

Nash stuffed two of the cucumber and peanut butter sandwiches into his mouth at once, noting that the bishop didn't move to take any. When he finished the sandwiches, he spoke. "I want to come back to the community." Nash expected the bishop to gasp or to act surprised, but he kept a perfectly straight face. *I suppose the bishop hears lots of strange things all the time*, he thought, *especially after people come back from rumspringa*.

At that point Mrs. Graber reappeared. "Oh, you're out here," she said, her face falling with disappointment. "I wondered why the place had suddenly gone quiet. I brought you both some onion and honey tea. Good for colds." Mrs. Graber deposited two steaming mugs and walked away slowly, looking back over her shoulder.

"I see." The bishop smiled at Nash. "I'm glad to hear you want to come back to the community, that's *gut* to hear. So you have enjoyed a long *rumspringa*?"

"Yes, a long one." Nash suddenly felt tongue tied, and took a sip of the onion and honey tea, which didn't taste anywhere near as bad as it sounded.

"And you want to return to the community and be baptized?" The bishop was smiling encouragingly.

Nash nodded. "Err, yes." *That's what I already said*, Nash thought.

"That is the way of it these days. People of the younger generation seem to be taking a longer time on *rumspringa* and joining the community later than we did back in my day." The bishop chuckled to himself.

Nash was slowly being put at ease. The bishop was not stern or forbidding. He seemed cheerful enough and not judgmental at all. He wasn't at all what Nash had expected.

"Are you ready to receive the instruction when instruction starts in the coming weeks?" When Nash nodded, the bishop said, "*Gut*, *gut*. Well, why don't you tell me about yourself?"

Nash supposed that the bishop was fishing for information, so he figured he might as well tell him everything. The bishop would find out sooner or later, and there was no point delaying the inevitable.

"I have a car. It's old, but I'll sell it of course." He pointed to the car.

The bishop nodded with a look of approval on his face. "You obviously can drive a buggy though. You haven't been away from your community that long. You do like horses, don't you?"

"Oh yes," said Nash hurriedly. "I spent all my money on them." Seeing the bishop frowning in confusion, Nash explained. "I mean racehorses, gambling, that sort of thing. I gambled a lot on the horses and I owe money to bookmakers. I suppose I can pay them back with the money I get for selling the car though." *And when I have enough money, I'll buy a fast, black harness horse, bigger, faster, and better looking than Jessie's black horse*, Nash thought gleefully, imagining how dashing he would look speeding up and down the dirt roads.

"Go on."

"What?" Nash came back to reality. "Oh, and I have tattoos and piercings. I won't put the piercings back in." Nash drew a breath and then continued. "I've been cruel and mean to people. I made my mother cry. I was horrible to Sarah Beachy and I told her she was a Miller. I'm kind to animals though."

Nash thought the bishop's mouth twitched slightly in amusement, but he couldn't be sure.

"Is there more?" asked the bishop.

Nash looked at the bishop carefully. He thought the bishop would have been impressed by his catalog of misdeeds, but the bishop seemed to think it was all a bit tame. Nash didn't know whether to be relieved or offended. "You don't think that's bad enough?" he asked.

"It's not what I think that matters," the bishop said. "It's what *Gott* thinks that matters. And what do you think, Nash? Do you think you have gone astray?"

"Why, yes, quite badly, I thought," Nash said. "Can I still get baptized?"

The bishop smiled, and then said, "All we like sheep have gone astray; we have turned every one to his own way; and the Lord hath laid on him the iniquity of us all."

Nash stared at the bishop. "So you mean we've *all* gone astray?"

"There is none righteous, no not one," the bishop quoted.

Nash nodded. "I see." He wondered if the bishop would quote Scripture in answer to all his questions. The bishop from his community never quoted Scripture, and in fact rebuked anyone who did, calling them *Scripture Smart* for pridefully showing off their knowledge of Scripture.

"The thing is," the bishop continued, "when someone is baptized and becomes a member of the community, he puts his old life behind him. You submit to *Gott*; you submit to the leaders, and you submit to the community. There is no going back. Can you do that, Nash?"

"Yes," Nash said confidently. "I've thought it all through. I don't think I can have a personality change overnight though, but I'll try my best."

The bishop leaned forward in his chair. "So, Nash, what prompted this change of heart?"

Nash shrugged. "I suppose you could say I've seen the error of my ways." He chuckled at his cliché.

The bishop did not look amused. "Would this have anything to do with a young lady from the community?"

Nash was horrified. "How did you know? Who told you?"

The bishop smiled. "No one told me, but it is often the case that young *menner* wish to return to the community because they want to marry a *maidel* from the community."

Nash nodded. "Oh, I see."

"So I hope that is not your only reason for returning to the community?"

"Oh no. I don't even think she likes me. She's a bit strange." Nash bit his lip, wondering if he had gone too far by criticizing someone to the bishop. "She's very nice and all, but I just can't figure her out."

The bishop suppressed a chuckle. "So the young lady has nothing to do with your wanting to return to the community."

Nash thought about it before answering. "She did make me have a long, hard look at myself, if that's what you mean, and I think that helped me want to return, but she's not the reason I want to come back. I want to come back for myself."

The bishop smiled. "*Gut*, Nash. I appreciate your honesty." He then held out the plate of raw liver and nettle sandwiches to Nash.

Nash looked at him through narrowed eyes, wondering if the bishop did, in fact, want to punish him. He politely declined. *Those* sandwiches he was not going to eat, free or not.

Chapter Eighteen

Sarah drove to town early in the morning. It was a lovely spring day, and spring was Sarah's favorite season. She loved the fragrance of all the flowers making their first appearance since the previous summer, and the feeling of anticipation in the air that spring always brought with it.

Sarah was on cloud nine. It seemed as if Benjamin did have feelings for her after all. Nevertheless, she did not want to get her hopes up, as he had still not asked her on a buggy ride. Was he waiting for her to say she would return home with him? An unpleasant thought suddenly niggled at her. What if he was pretending to like her so she would return to her *daed*? After all, her *daed* had sent Benjamin to fetch her back. Had Benjamin been reporting back to her *daed* all this time?

Sarah shook her head in disbelief. Surely Benjamin wasn't like that. He was honest and trustworthy and kind. Yet why would he act as if he liked her but not ask her on a buggy ride? It just didn't make sense.

Sarah tied up her horse not far from Mrs. Hostetler's store and carefully unloaded the Spinning Star quilt from the buggy. She had been sewing for Mrs. Hostetler for some time now, and was still worried that her sewing might not be good enough, despite Mrs. Hostetler's assurances to the contrary.

Mrs. Hostetler was busy with an early customer, so Sarah waited in the back room. Mrs. Hostetler joined her soon after, and gushed over her sewing ability. "Why, Sarah, this is beautiful work as usual. Your sewing is very fine."

Sarah blushed furiously. She had been brought up to believe that compliments were improper as they led to vainglory and pride. Still, Mrs. Miller had told her more than once with stern disapproval that Mrs. Hostetler was "fast," meaning she was not strict.

"Sarah, have you thought any more about coming to work for me three days a week?"

Sarah nodded. "*Jah*, but I worry about Mrs. Miller being all alone with all Hannah, Esther and Martha married, and Rebecca and Mary soon to be married as well."

"Mrs. Miller will be alone when you get married though."

Sarah blushed again. "*Nee*, I don't think I'll ever get married, Mrs. Hostetler." *Not if I can't have Benjamin*, she thought. *I don't see how I can ever feel about someone else the way I feel about Benjamin.*

"Call me Katie, please."

Sarah simply nodded, a little embarrassed at Mrs. Hostetler's forward ways, and at the thought of marriage.

Mrs. Hostetler stopped talking to Sarah to attend to another customer. Sarah stood there awkwardly, and then turned her attention to a Log Cabin quilt, a wall hanging. She admired the work that had gone into the little rustic cabin, and the vivid blues, russets, greens.

Sarah idly looked out the big window. To her surprise, she saw Benjamin on the other side of the street, and with him was an Amish girl. Sarah's heart beat out of her chest. Who was that Amish girl?

"How could this be?" Sarah realized she had said the words aloud when Mrs. Hostetler shot her a puzzled look. Sarah dug her fingers into her apron and sank back into the recesses of the wall. It seemed as though she had stopped breathing. She peeked out the large window once more. Benjamin's hair blazed copper golden under his hat, and she admired his broad shoulders and the bulging, well-defined, muscles in his arms.

The girl turned around to gesture to something and Sarah saw it was Jessie Yoder. *What are Jessie and Benjamin doing with each other?* she thought. Her breath came in short bursts, and she felt as though she might faint. *Pull yourself together*, she silently scolded herself.

Sarah continued to watch. Was Benjamin attracted to Jessie? Were they there together or was this a chance meeting? She had no idea, and their body language really wasn't giving anything away one way or another.

Finally, Jessie laughed and then walked in one direction, while Benjamin smiled, gave a little wave, and walked in the other.

I don't think I've ever seen Jessie smile at anyone, Sarah thought with growing disquiet. *She did seem awfully friendly with Benjamin. I wonder what that was all about?* She felt quite put out.

As soon as the customer left, Sarah made to speak with Mrs. Hostetler, when another lady came through the door. This lady was interested in buying one of the Album Quilts. Its background was predominately white, with a little green and more red. Katie told her that the Album Quilt was hand sewn and that it was an example of the Baltimore Album Quilt most popular from the 1840s to the 1890s.

After the lady paid for the quilt and left, someone else entered the store. This time it was Mark. "*Hullo, Aenti* Katie," he said.

Sarah had forgotten for a moment that Mrs. Hostetler was Mark's aunt.

"Mark!" Mrs. Hostetler exclaimed with delight, giving him a big hug.

Sarah was aware her mouth had fallen open. The Amish in her community were not given to public displays of affection. Mark hugged his aunt back, so Sarah figured the whole Hostetler *familye* must have forward ways indeed.

"So Mark, how are you enjoying your time with the Miller *familye*?"

"It's *gut*," Mark said and then caught sight of Sarah. "*Hiya*, Sarah. Sorry, I didn't notice you there at first."

"I'm trying to talk Sarah into coming to work for me," Mrs. Hostetler said. "I've offered her a job."

Sarah simply nodded.

"How's Beth?" Mark asked Sarah. "Is she here with you?"

Sarah shook her head. "*Nee*, she and Mary have gone to the Yoders to play with the dog."

Mark nodded slowly. "Ah. I thought the three of us could have coffee." His face fell. "Oh well, never mind."

Sarah noticed a small smile playing on the corners of Mrs. Hostetler's lips, and she felt the same way. It seemed Mark had a little crush on Beth. That was quite a relief to Sarah. She knew Beth was worried that she had not yet found a man and that Beth felt she never would. Beth had often shared with her how she despaired of ever finding a good *mann* and of ever having *kinner*, but maybe the answer was right here in the person of Mark Hostetler.

But how did Beth feel about Mark? When she had pressed her, Beth had become speechless. It wasn't like her. She was sure Beth was keeping something from her. But what? It wasn't like Beth at all. The two of them always shared confidences.

Besides, Sarah had noticed Beth was seemed different when Mark was around. At first she had thought her friend was developing feelings for Mark and so felt embarrassed when she was around him, but more recently she had caught Beth glaring at him.

In fact, if she didn't know better, she would say Beth was resentful of Mark. But what possible reason could there be? She knew there was no point questioning Beth about him as she would just fall silent as she always did whenever she brought up the subject of Mark.

Sarah rubbed her forehead and watched on as Mrs. Hostetler and Mark chatted away happily. Finally, Sarah promised to give the offered job some more thought, and left the store hurriedly.

It was still early, and Sarah had only consumed half a mug of *kaffi* in her rush that morning. She wondered whether or not to buy some *kaffi* and something to eat, but her stomach rumbled and made the decision for her.

There was a little café near Mrs. Hostetler's store. Sarah had been there several times before. The outside appearance was of a shabby appearance and gray. That, and the fact that there was a trendy café just down the street, made this café an unpopular place for tourists, and that was to Sarah's liking.

Inside the feel was homely, with the exposed brick walls, family atmosphere, and vintage wooden tables and chairs. There were no hurried businessmen or bustling, loud tourists here.

Sarah took a seat at the back of the café, facing out. There were no views as such, as the walls were brick rather than the floor to ceiling glass walls of the rival cafés on the street. Still, Sarah had not come here for a view; she had come for good *kaffi*, something to eat, and to have time to herself to think.

The aroma of roasted *kaffi* beans filled the air. It was a welcoming scent, which reminded her of the Miller *haus* first thing in the morning.

Sarah ordered Eggs Benedict and *kaffi*, and sat looking at the menu, just for somewhere to rest her eyes while she thought. When her *kaffi* was served, she looked up to see Benjamin sitting further to the front of the café. Her stomach immediately twisted into a tight knot. *How long has he been there?* she wondered. Tentatively, she gave a little wave.

Benjamin waved back, and then stood up and made his way over to her.

"*Hiya*, Benjamin, I didn't see you come in."

Benjamin smiled. "I was here first, and you walked straight past me."

Sarah's hand flew to her mouth. "I did? Sorry, Benjamin, I only just noticed you then." Benjamin looked a little hurt, so Sarah hurried to add, "I was daydreaming, off in my own world."

Benjamin smiled. "That's all right. May I join you? Oh, unless you're expecting someone else?"

Is he jealous? Sarah wondered, very much hoping that he was. "*Nee*, please join me," she said. After an interval, she said, "So, are you here alone?"

Benjamin chuckled. "Not now, as you're here with me."

Sarah felt her cheeks burn. "*Nee*, it's just that I saw you with Jessie Yoder earlier." She said it in the most

even tone she could muster. After all, she did not want
Benjamin to suspect she was jealous.

Benjamin seemed puzzled. "Jessie? Oh yes, I happened upon her. She was telling me something funny
that happened with a guest this morning."

"Oh?" Sarah waited patiently for Benjamin to tell
her the funny incident, but he remained silent. *Did
he make that up?* she wondered.

Sarah was about to ask, when the waiter arrived
with her Eggs Benedict. Benjamin ordered some more
kaffi for himself. "I've already eaten," he explained.
"What are you doing in town this morning?"

Sarah was embarrassed that Benjamin had asked
her a question when her mouth was full. She pointed
to her mouth to indicate that she'd have to eat her
mouthful before answering, and Benjamin nodded.
"I was bringing a quilt I'd finished to Mrs. Hostetler,"
she said after a minute or two. "Mrs. Hostetler wants
me to work for her three days a week, but I don't
want to leave Mrs. Miller alone. After all, three of
her *dochders* are all married, and Rebecca and Mary
will be soon, so Mrs. Miller would be terribly lonely
if I wasn't there every day."

Benjamin nodded his thanks to the waiter who had
just brought his *kaffi*, and then said, "But you'll have
to leave her sometime, like when you get married."

"That's what Mrs. Hostetler said too," Sarah said
automatically, but then felt a slow flush travel up her
cheeks, and hung her head slightly, hoping the light
was too dim for Benjamin to see her blushing.

Why was he mentioning marriage? It was one

thing for Mrs. Hostetler to mention marriage, but not Benjamin. "What are you doing here?" Sarah asked, to try to cover up how she was feeling.

"Well, I have some news," Benjamin said, likewise looking a little embarrassed.

"You do?" Sarah was worried he would tell her he was getting married. She bit her lip and held her breath.

"I haven't mentioned it before."

Sarah nodded, wishing he'd come to the point in a hurry.

"As you know, Mr. Miller has a furniture making business and his retail outlet is nearby. They gave me a tour of the retail store this morning, and I start next week as an apprentice carpenter."

Sarah was shocked. Of everything she imagined that Benjamin was about to say, this was not one of the options. "Why, why?" she sputtered.

"I don't want to be a farmer like my *vadder* and his *vadder* before him. I want to have my own B&B one day, but I like furniture, and this will allow me to build up an income so I can afford a B&B later on."

Sarah shook her head. "I mean, why here? This means that you're not going back home."

"*Nee*," Benjamin said, smiling at her tenderly. "How do you feel about that?"

"Me? Me?" Sarah spluttered, her emotions all in turmoil and suddenly wondering where her ability to speak had gone. "Err, that would be *gut*. I'd like it if you stayed here," she added boldly. *What do I have to lose?* she thought. *Maybe he hasn't asked me on a buggy ride as he isn't sure if I like him.*

Benjamin simply smiled widely in reply.

Yet, despite the big hint Sarah considered she had given Benjamin, there was no mention of a buggy ride, despite the two spending the next hour in amicable conversation.

Chapter Nineteen

The soft sunlight shining in faintly through the windows was enough to rustle Beth from her disturbed slumber. She rubbed away the weariness from her eyes as she sat up in her bed, still fighting to stay awake. Beth had tossed and turned all night, and through the night went to the kitchen three times for a glass of water. She arose before five, and kept pacing. Finally, she decided she would ask Mark Hostetler if he had, in fact, cruelly abandoned Miriam Hilty. Otherwise, she felt she would go quite mad.

After Beth dressed, she made her way toward the kitchen to make some *kaffi*. As she sat there, waiting for it to brew, she wondered whether she really should question him. Would a liar tell the truth when pressed?

Breakfast tasted like cardboard, but Beth forced some down. She could imagine her stomach growling embarrassingly while talking to Mark if she did not. While she was still deciding what to do, she heard the patter of footsteps making its way toward her. Moments later, Mrs. Miller walked in.

"*Guten mariye!*" She pulled out a seat at the table beside Beth. "There's a lot that needs to get done around the *haus* today, so I was wondering if you would go into town for groceries with Mark. I made a list, but if the two of you would go for me, I can stay here and get everything cleaned and ready."

Oh no, another day with Mark? Beth felt slightly repulsed, but she didn't want to seem rude in any way. "Of course. I'd be happy to," she said, looking away in hopes of hiding her apprehension.

When she turned, however, Mark was stepping into the kitchen wearing the most annoying smile she had seen on his face all week. "It looks like I'm just in time for some *kaffi*," he said, seeming a bit too cheerful for that time of the morning, especially for one who had not yet had *kaffi*.

"You are, indeed," Mrs. Miller said. "We were just talking. Would you mind taking Beth into town to get the list of groceries?"

"That wouldn't be a problem at all. I'd be happy to," he said, sounding sincere.

Of course he would, she thought. *Anything to bother me for another day.* Instead of wallowing in self-pity, however, Beth decided to embrace the day completely. Even with Mark by her side, nothing was going to hold her back from enjoying herself.

When the *kaffi* was finally done brewing, she filled three mugs carefully and then passed one to Mrs. Miller and another to Mark. Beth then looked down at her mug as she cradled it in her hands, the steam billowing toward her face with a wonderful aroma. After taking a sip of the warm beverage, she looked up to see Mark watching her. He immediately averted eye contact, but she had already caught him staring. Why couldn't he just avoid looking at her? Every time he looked at her, the stories that Miriam had told her about him were all that she could think of, and it tore her up inside.

Beth was able to keep her frustrations in check as thoughts of dinner flashed by. She could already smell the cookies and freshly baked bread, along with the mashed potatoes and gravy. Even though she had reason enough to let Mark's presence bother her, the idea of spending time with her *gut* friend, Sarah, made it worth it. "After *kaffi*, I will go get ready so we can make the trip into town," she said, just before taking a second sip.

"Okay, and I'll ready the horse and buggy in the meantime," Mark said, not missing a beat. Beth glared at him, not sure whether she wanted to thank him or say something rude.

"*Denki*," Mrs. Miller said, unknowingly silencing Beth before her snide remark could be uttered.

"Whatever you need," Mark said, lifting his cup to his lips and draining it. He then slid it onto the table and headed outside.

After the door closed behind him, Mrs. Miller looked up at Beth and chuckled. "*Menner* from some other Amish communities appear to be a little strange to my way of thinking. Regardless, he sure does seem like a *gut mann* though. What do you think?"

"Possibly," Beth said, hoping to avoid another conversation about Mark and being matched with him.

"Perhaps you're seeing something that I am missing, but I rarely ever make mistakes when it comes to these things," Mrs. Miller said, her tone serious.

Beth remembered Sarah's stance on her aunt's matchmaking and almost laughed aloud, but was able to hold it in. "Well, I trust your judgment, but I should get ready so we can go get those groceries for you."

Mrs. Miller nodded. "Here is the money for them," she said, handing it to her before sending Beth off to get prepared.

After Beth finished getting ready and had tied her bonnet perfectly, she headed back to the kitchen to retrieve the shopping list. Mrs. Miller was already in the process of cleaning, only looking back to point toward the piece of paper on the table. "Everything we need is on there, so please try not to forget anything."

"I won't," Beth said, taking the list before going outside.

When she stepped outside, Beth saw Mark standing beside the buggy. As she approached, he pulled open the door and extended his hand to help her. *More false displays of polite behavior*, she thought, shaking her head as she reluctantly took his hand and climbed up into the vehicle.

Moments later, Mark was in the driver's seat, moving his hands gently. With a quick jolt, the horse sprang into motion, causing the scenery to degrade into a blur as they drove at a strong trot toward town. "So, might I ask how you've been enjoying your holiday so far?"

Beth had been so keen to speak with Mark, but now she was dumbstruck. Maybe she would not be able to bring up the subject of Miriam after all. She turned to him and shook her head. "I've enjoyed staying with the Millers, but I could definitely have done without…"

"Without what?" he said, scrunching his brow.

"Oh, nothing," she said, looking back out her window. She knew that Mark wouldn't want to hear the real answer, and now she had no desire to be that inconsiderate, even if he did deserve it.

"I'm not quite sure what you meant, but I hope whatever it is soon changes for the better," he said, as the buggy turned into the market's parking lot.

After tying up the horse, Mark walked over and helped Beth down. "*Denki*," she said, brushing off her apron before heading inside the store.

Beth took a shopping cart and began searching for the items on her list. It was longer than she had initially thought, but it did make sense since the Millers' *schweschders* and their *familyes* would all be at the house for dinner that evening.

Slowly checking off each grocery on the list, Beth found herself alone. Where had Mark gone? Did her cold demeanor in the buggy cause him distress, or was he just being his true self for once and not helping? As she hoisted two large chickens into the cart, she let out a long, drawn-out sigh in disgust.

"Do you need help with those?" a familiar voice asked. When she turned around, she saw Mark standing beside his own cart.

Beth immediately felt her chest tightening as anger threatened to overwhelm her. *Of course I needed help*, she thought. "Oh, it's okay," she said aloud. "I could have certainly used some help, but I managed without it. And what are those for?" she asked, pointing to items that filled his cart. "Those things are not on Mrs. Miller's list, and even if they were, I have it, so you couldn't have possibly known."

Mark's brow furrowed, like he was unsure of what to say—or perhaps he was just afraid, but of what? Was he hiding something again? "I figured there'd be no harm in doing some separate shopping while we were in town. Is that okay?"

"Sure," Beth said, quickly looking away as a feeling of shame washed over her. As long as he didn't expect to use Mrs. Miller's money on his groceries, it wasn't an issue, but for some reason, Beth felt uneasy about it.

"*Gut*," he said, peering into her cart. "Do you think those chickens will be big enough to feed everyone?"

Beth glared at him, shaking her head slightly. "Yes, I think they are fine. If you'd like to actually help me this time, however, I would implore you to stay close," she said, pushing her cart down the aisle at a brisk pace.

As she slowly found everything on the list, Mark stayed by her side to help. She could tell that he felt guilty about leaving her alone in the beginning, but was it just another ploy to garner sympathy from her? Probably, she thought, as she headed toward the registers to cash out.

Beth began putting the groceries up on the counter as the woman behind the register smiled. "Good morning! Did you find everything you were looking for?"

"Yes, thank you," she said, continuing to unload her things as the clerk rang through the items.

When Beth reached in for the chickens, Mark looked at her and shook his head. "I'll get them," he said, lifting not only the chickens but all the heavy items for her.

After paying the clerk, Beth pushed her cart out into the open foyer as she waited for Mark to cash his items out. She watched carefully to see what he had bought, but it looked like the normal odds and ends for any dinner. There was even a large chicken that looked like it might only feed two or three people. Who was he buying that food for? It made little sense. Her curiosity got the best of her.

"Who are those for?" she whispered, stepping close to him as he pulled the money from his own wallet.

Mark glanced up immediately, but his soft eyes looked pained. "They're just for a friend."

Beth scratched her head, still unsure of what was going on. Who was this "friend" that he had all of a sudden? And why would he be spending his own, hard-earned money on someone else's groceries? Once Mark had finished cashing out, they headed back to the buggy, where he unloaded the contents of both carts into the back before heading back home.

The ride back was a bit more awkward than the ride there had been. Now, instead of a strained conversation, there was nothing but silence, and a tension so palpable she could almost touch it.

As they left town, they also left the unpleasant sounds and smells of the city behind and Beth took in the scent of the spicebush, the milkweed, and untainted country air. There was a gentle breeze, and Beth could not but help admire the wildflowers, the pink moccasin flowers, and the bladdernut with its lily-of-the-valley-like flowers sprouting from rocks.

When Beth could see the Millers' *haus* in the distance, she let out a long sigh of relief. She could finally breathe without feeling trapped and confused. It still bothered her that Mark was being secretive, but at least she wouldn't be alone with him anymore that day—or so she hoped.

Mark parked the buggy, but didn't return the horse to the barn as he usually did. Beth found it very odd, but after their journey into town, it seemed that was par for the course that day. He helped unload all the groceries except his own, and carried them inside for her.

"You're back already?" Mrs. Miller said, sounding pleased. "I hope you got everything on the list."

"We did," Mark said, speaking before Beth could, "but may I ask you a favor? May I use your buggy to run an errand? I won't be long."

Mrs. Miller nodded. "Of course you may."

Mark smiled and thanked her before walking back outside. Beth just stood there, trying to make sense of the curious *mann*. What was his deal, and why was he so mysterious all of a sudden?

Chapter Twenty

As Beth walked down the hall, she heard several
familiar voices congregating there. Upon entering
the room, she saw that Hannah's *familye* and Esther's
familye were already there, but the others had yet to
arrive. She headed to the sofa and sat down beside
Sarah and Benjamin, looking over at Mr. and Mrs.
Miller.

She hadn't even noticed him at first, but Mark was
by the hearth as well. He did not look up or greet her,
instead focusing mostly on the small kitten he held
tightly to him. Beth wanted to say something to him
in order to evoke a response, but she knew it would
come off as rude and insensitive, and even if he did
deserve it, that would be crossing the line.

Sarah turned to her. "The others should be here
soon."

In a matter of about fifteen minutes, the family
room had gone from spacious and partially empty to
full. Mr. Miller rose, with an old, thick book in his

hand. He flipped to a specific page and began to read from it. As he did, Beth listened carefully, until right after he said something that affected her greatly. "*If anyone wrongs you, exercise a forgiving spirit and patiently dismiss the matter. For if you take the wrong to heart and become angry, you hurt no one but yourself and only do what your enemy wants you to do. If, however, you patiently forgive him, Gott will in his own good time judge the evildoer and bring your innocence to light.*"

As his voice softly faded from Beth's focus, all she could think of was the message that was being delivered. She was accustomed to hearing similar prayers and devotions daily, but for some reason, she found herself staring at Mark as those words were read. As her chest tightened, she wondered if she would ever be able to forgive him. Try after try, she just kept failing at it, and it pained her immensely. If only he would apologize or something, it might not be so difficult.

A gentle knock interrupted the conversation. Mrs. Miller headed out to answer the front door, and came back with Mrs. Ramseyer.

"Excuse me please, we have a guest," Mrs. Miller said, calling for everyone's attention. "Rhoda Ramseyer is here."

Rhoda Ramseyer spoke in a soft, meek voice as she presented two cakes. "I wanted to thank the Millers for all the help they've given me after my husband went to be with *Der Herr*. I made this cake for you all," she said, handing the first to Mr. Miller.

"And this is for Mr. Mark Hostetler," she said, walking over toward the *mann* who was still sitting with his kitten by the fire. "I heard you love Shoo-fly pie, so I made this one for you. *Denki* again."

Mark stood up to receive his gift, with his purring feline in one hand. He then extended the other to accept it, and thanked her. "You didn't need to do that," he said with a smile. "*Denki.*"

"Rhoda, would you like to join us for dinner?" Mrs. Miller said.

"*Jah, denki,*" Rhoda said, "but I must decline. I have some things to take care of."

"Then what about tomorrow? Please call by whenever you're free," Mrs. Miller said, leading her out of the room.

Beth sat there, surprised. Why did Mrs. Ramseyer give Mark a special gift? She had helped just as much as he had, and so had Sarah and Benjamin. It was most puzzling. As the seconds ticked by, the fluttering in her stomach got worse. She needed to find out why Mark had been singled out like that by Mrs. Ramseyer. There had to be an explanation.

Beth stood up and headed toward the front door. She passed by the kitchen to see that Mrs. Miller had stopped in to check on the food, so she decided to see if Mrs. Ramseyer was still on the property. Rushing outside, she saw Mrs. Ramseyer climbing into her buggy. Beth ran to her and called out, "Please, wait!"

Mrs. Ramseyer turned around, her body half inside the buggy. "Oh, Beth. I hadn't seen you. Is there something you need?"

"Actually," she replied, gasping for air from the short run. "I was just curious as to why you made Mark a special pie."

"Oh," the woman said, her smile fading. "Well, he made me promise not to tell anyone…"

What? Beth couldn't comprehend what she meant. What could he possibly be hiding in regard to Mrs. Ramseyer? It made absolutely no sense—until Mrs. Ramseyer spoke again.

"Mark stopped by with his hands full of groceries for me. I couldn't believe how generous and helpful he had been. First, you all came to help, and then that. I just felt that I had to repay his kindness somehow. Please, don't tell him that I told you though," Mrs. Ramseyer added, her tone somewhat guilty.

"I won't," Beth said. "*Denki*, Mrs. Ramseyer."

As the buggy drove away, Beth stood there, her mouth open in shock. What was going on? Was that why Mark had bought all of those groceries, and with his own money? She could understand the gesture, just not from someone like him. Mark really didn't seem anything like Miriam had described him.

Beth headed back inside, but her mood had changed entirely. No longer was she so upbeat. She just wanted to know what was really going on with Mark. As she walked into the room again, Beth saw the children playing together. Their happy chatter lifted her spirits.

When she sat down beside Sarah once again, her friend must have picked up on her change of mood. "Is something wrong? And where did you go?"

"It's nothing," she said, her gaze focused on Mark again. Not only did he help a lonely woman, but he was so kind and nurturing to that kitten.

"I've known you long enough to know that isn't the case," Sarah said. "You've been weird around Mark since the first day he showed up, but now you're acting even stranger and he seems to be avoiding you. What is it that I'm not aware of?"

Beth swallowed the lump in her throat before slowly turning her attention to Sarah. "If you truly want to know, it's about what he did to my friend, Miriam. He is a cruel, hard, cold *mann* who jilted her terribly. I've tried so hard not to hold a grudge, but it's been rather impossible with the way he's been acting."

Sarah scratched her head as a strange expression crossed on her face. "Jilted? You wouldn't happen to mean Miriam Hilty, would you?"

Beth was shocked. "Actually, yes. How did you know?"

"Miss Hilty has been known for her loose handling of the truth," Sarah said with a shake of her head. "The woman appears convinced that most *menner* in the community have wronged her in one way or another. I assure you that these are just the ramblings of an envious girl. Miriam probably just had a big crush on Mark and was too ashamed to admit that was as far as it ever got. I promise you, from what I know of the Hostetlers and Mark himself, I can confidently tell you that he is neither cruel, cold, nor hard in any way. Just look at how he's been taking care of that kitten. He's a kind, gentle *mann*."

Beth then looked back over at Mark, wondering whom to believe. Miriam had been a friend for a long time, but would that stop her from stretching the truth to such a degree? And then there was Sarah, who would not lie, and her words rang all too true. If Beth had never heard Mark's name before meeting him, she never would have seen him in any sort of negative light.

Maybe Sarah was right. Come to think of it, her other friends had said that Miriam always took liberties with the truth, but she had never imagined Miriam would tell such a complicated lie about Mark Hostetler.

"Oh my," Beth said, gasping at the realization. She then looked back at Sarah and shook her head. "I never would have imagined that Miriam would lie to me like that. I should have talked with you about it sooner."

"I don't know what Miriam's intentions were, but please don't believe her lies at all. I wish you'd told me sooner and I could have set you straight. Miriam Hilty and I are not from the same community, but I've heard all about her. Perhaps you should give Mark another chance. Just don't let my aunt hear that I said such a thing," Sarah said.

"Maybe you're right," Beth said, her cheeks warming as a lump formed in the back of her throat.

The morning had gone fairly well, other than Beth's realization that Miriam had been lying to her all along. Now, she sat at the kitchen table, waiting for dinner to begin. Even though the entire *familye* was there, Beth found herself at a loss for words due to her dreadful and unfair behavior toward Mark. With Sarah's revelation, she had learned the truth, but how could she possibly atone for how she acted?

"Please be seated everyone," Mrs. Miller called out, her voice loud and stern. "And *kinner* as well. You'll have more time to play later."

Beth sat quietly, her mind in such a deep fog that all she saw was the table of food before her. She could still hear the noise and chatter around the table, but it sounded muffled and unintelligible.

The dinner looked delectable, and there were so many delicious things to choose from. Bowls of mashed potatoes and gravy sat beside the creamed celery dish, along with some pickled cabbage and homemade applesauce. The aroma of freshly baked bread mixed with something savory tickled her nose.

Then, Beth noticed what that savory smell was. It was the two chickens sitting in the table's center, the ones she had bought at the store when she was with Mark. It reminded her of his selfless and caring deed for Mrs. Ramseyer. *Oh great*, she thought. *Even the food is making me feel bad.*

"Thank you for coming to our home," Mr. Miller said. He then glanced down for the silent prayer.

Beth closed her eyes and bowed her head. Instead of silently reciting the Lord's Prayer as she was so accustomed to doing before dinners, she needed to personalize it this time.

Our Father, I seek from you forgiveness, that which I was unable to offer, when I felt it was needed.

Now, however, I know that it is I who needs to be for-given. Please, give me the strength and courage to apologize to the person who deserves it most.

Just as she finished, Beth heard several exhales around her. Opening her eyes slowly, she noticed that the others had finished their silent prayers as well.

"Please, enjoy the food," Mrs. Miller said.

With that, the adults filled plates for their *kinner* who sat together at the little table.

Everyone filled their plates of food and ate, with soft conversation sparking up around the table. Not long after, Mark sat beside Beth. She gave him a small smile.

"I'm sorry if you didn't want me sitting near you, but it's the last seat available. I had to take the kitten to a back room before I could join you all."

"Oh," she replied, swallowing hard. "Have you tried the baked corn?"

"I haven't yet, but I will now that you've vouched for it," he said, offering her a smile before quickly averting his gaze.

Beth wanted to tell him how sorry she was for what had happened, but it just wasn't the right place or time. Yet would there ever be a good time to admit to her appalling behavior? She had been rude, inconsiderate, and rather snide at times. Back then, Beth had been convinced Mark deserved it. Now, however, she knew otherwise. She was thoroughly ashamed of herself.

Mrs. Miller turned to Beth and Mark. "Before everyone leaves, would you two care to fetch some more mint leaves for tea?"

Beth's face fell. Her first thought was, *Oh no, here we go again*, but her mood quickly changed. She realized that it would be the perfect opportunity to come clean to Mark and let him know how sorry she was for how she had been treating him. Her stomach churned at the thought of speaking with him, but she had to do it. Through the fear and worry and no doubt, embarrassment, she had to do it.

Mark turned to her and narrowed his eyes. "Are you sure?"

"Yes," she said, smiling back at him. "I am."

He nodded and stood to his feet before extending his hand to help her up. Beth went to the kitchen to fetch the basket they had used last time, and then the two headed outside. Mark pulled the front door open, holding it for her. Just as she stepped out onto the porch, a soft purring sound caused her to look down. There was the kitten, running between her legs to get outside. She tried to reach for her, but stumbled, letting the cat escape down the steps.

"Come back!" Mark called out, pulling the door shut before chasing after the kitten.

Beth immediately darted after the kitten. The little kitten made her way all the way to the first buggy in the yard before she caught her. Beth scooped her up and scolded her gently. "You have to be careful out here! It's—"

Right then, Mark ran up to her, extending his hands toward the kitten. His eyes seemed softer than usual, but the look on his face showed how scared he had been. Taking the kitten into his arms, he stroked her softly. "Don't ever do that again please," he said, his voice soft and shaky. "*Denki* for saving her, Beth."

"I didn't save her," Beth said, shaking her head. "You did. You saved her when she mysteriously showed up on the porch. You saved her by showing her love and affection when whoever abandoned her wouldn't. You save a lot of people, I think."

Mark shook his head. "I don't understand…"

"Shall we take her inside before fetching that mint?" Beth asked.

"Yes, I will now. I don't know how she got out though. I didn't see her at all when I opened the door," Mark said, his voice filled with remorse.

"It's okay. She's fine now," Beth said.

"I really don't like calling her 'she,' but I didn't want to seem rude and selfish naming her by myself. Would you care to do the honor? I think she likes you," Mark said, lifting the kitten toward Beth.

"Oh, well maybe that's something that we can discuss later," Beth said, not wanting to make such a big decision without putting thought into it.

"That sounds *gut*," Mark said, turning back toward the house. "I'll be right back."

Beth stood there, glancing toward the garden patch. The wind was bitter now, causing goose pimples to line every bit of her skin. Or was that just her nerves?

Moments later, Mark appeared beside her again. "Shall we get that mint now?"

Beth nodded. She followed him as they walked over to the small, leafy area of the property. The wildflowers growing around the area gave the otherwise dark green patch of land some vibrant color, but that wasn't the beauty Beth was focused on now. "Mark, may I be honest with you about something?" she asked, just as he was kneeling down by a tall mint plant.

"Sure," he said, staring up at her.

"I'm certain you've noticed that I've been rather distant around you since the day you arrived here. I wanted to apologize for that. I should have come to you sooner and just asked you the truth. Instead, I believed in a friend who I just learned cannot be trusted. Please forgive me," Beth said, swallowing hard.

"I don't know if I understand. Who was your friend, and what did he or she tell you about me?"

"Her name is Miriam Hilty. She told me that the two of you were engaged, and that you jilted her with no explanation, leaving her heartbroken and alone. I never had any reason to doubt her, but when you showed up and I saw the real you, I should have known. I do know the truth now though."

Mark then stood up and looked right into her eyes. "Miriam Hilty told you that? I have heard of her, but I don't know her any better than any other girl in the nearby community. She's not from my community. I promise you, I never hurt her like that and I certainly wasn't engaged to her. Like I said, I barely even know her. I would never..."

"I know," Beth said. "I know. And that's why I felt

so bad about how I've been acting. Please forgive me. I just wish it wasn't too late now to get to know you."

Mark shook his head as his face broke into a wide grin. "It's never too late. I'm glad that we both know the truth now. I just hope we can always keep it that way."

"Always?" Beth asked, unsure of what he meant by it.

"Yes, always, or so I hope. Beth, would you be interested in joining me for a buggy ride?"

Beth gasped. Why was it so easy for him to forgive her, when she had struggled so much with forgiving him? And he had even asked her on a buggy ride! When she first saw him, she had felt an immediate attraction, but she had held a wrongful opinion of him ever since, until Sarah had set her straight. Finally, she found her voice. "*Jah*, I would love to. I really would."

Mark smiled. "*Wunderbar*! I can't wait," he said shyly.

Suddenly, a loud roar erupted from a small bush just a few yards away from the garden patch. The leaves shook as a small boy emerged with his arms flailing and his mouth open wide. "I'm telling!" he yelled, before rushing toward the front of the *haus*.

Beth stood there in shock for what felt like an eternity. Then, she turned to Mark and sighed. "Hannah's *sohn* is going to tell everyone what we just talked about."

"Then we had better get inside," Mark said with

a smile, putting the last of the mint leaves into the basket. "Come on."

"How about Patch," Beth said, "for a name? It matches the kitten's fur, and it describes a special place for us."

Mark nodded. "I love it. We can tell the kitten her new name together. First however, we might have to answer a few questions," he said with a chuckle.

When they returned inside, they were both met with bulging eyes and wide smiles. "Is it true?" Sarah said, her voice sounding hopeful. "Are you both really going on a buggy ride?"

"*Jah*," Mark said, smiling at Beth. "It's true."

"See, I told you!" Mrs. Miller said, throwing her hands up. "Yet another marriage that has come about with my help. And you all say I'm not *gut* at this!"

Everyone collapsed into helpless laughter.

Chapter Twenty-One

Sarah and Mrs. Miller were at the mud sale held to raise money for the local volunteer fire department. There were thousands of people present, and Sarah didn't like crowds. Still, Mr. Miller served on the volunteer firefighting crews, as did all the Hostetler *bruders*, so Mrs. Miller wanted to attend.

Sarah stepped gingerly over the muddy fields. "I know why it gets its name," she said to Mrs. Miller.

"It's not bad this year, as we haven't had so much rain," Mrs. Miller said. "Anyway, the earlier mud sales are much worse, due to the thawing snow. We might have rain today, if those clouds are any indication."

Sarah looked up at the ominous thunderclouds gathering at a rapid pace, and then turned her attention back to the mud sale. Sarah found the chaos disconcerting. There were tents, and she heard the call of several different auctioneers at once. She followed Mrs. Miller past horses going into the tent to be auctioned, and past tents filled with quilts. Everywhere she looked, people were inspecting items ranging from buggies to farming equipment, lumber, furniture, produce, baked goods, antiques, housewares and all manner of handmade crafts as well as a strange variety of livestock.

Both women stopped to admire a traditional English hexagon quilt. Sarah looked at the work that had gone into the pretty blue and lavender patchwork quilt. It was constructed entirely of hundreds of small, hand-pieced hexagons, pieced together to form patchwork "flowers." She knew each hexagon had been made by basting fabric to a hexagonal paper template, before all the hexagons were hand stitched to each other. The basting and templates were then removed from inner hexagons, leaving the outer row of hexagons intact. Half flowers edged the quilt top.

Mrs. Miller, clearly experienced at mud sales, led Sarah to a striped white and bright yellow tent, which they walked through to reach the fire hall. To Sarah's delight, food was served in the fire hall. Both she and Mrs. Miller had missed breakfast that morning, as they had to do an entire day's chores before leaving for the mud sale.

Sarah bought chicken corn soup, and Mrs. Miller chose pot pie. Both women also bought *kaffi*. They found a seat in the corner of the room. Sarah was relieved to sit down and catch a moment's respite away from the hustle and bustle of the crowds. She overheard someone say that there were twenty thousand people in attendance, and she was not surprised, not that she had ever seen so many people in the one place, Amish and *Englischers* alike. They were not strolling around casually; each person seemed intent on finding a bargain.

Soon both Mrs. Miller and Sarah were each tucking into a sticky bun. Sarah thought again how blessed she was to be with the Miller *familye*. Mrs. Miller treated her like one of her own *dochders*.

Mrs. Miller hurried to finish her mouthful, and said, "Why, look, Sarah, there's Benjamin Shetler." Mrs. Miller waved him over.

The old feeling of butterflies arose in Sarah's stomach when she saw Benjamin, who walked toward them holding a funnel pie. "*Hullo*, Mrs. Miller. *Hiya*, Sarah."

Sarah's heart thumped loudly when he spoke to her, and she smiled and dropped her eyes.

"Sit with us, Benjamin," Mrs. Miller said. It was a command rather than an invitation, and Benjamin sat down at once.

"I didn't know you would be here, Benjamin." Sarah was worried that Benjamin would think she was following him. Sarah knew it was likely an unreasonable thought, but people in love are sometimes given to unreasonable thoughts.

"I serve on the volunteer firefighting crew."

Mrs. Miller nodded her approval, and Sarah said, "I didn't know that."

Benjamin smiled at her, and tingles ran all through Sarah.

Mrs. Miller's hand suddenly flew to her mouth.

"Oh, I forgot there was something I had to do. I won't be long. Benjamin, would you mind staying with Sarah until I return?"

Without waiting for an answer, Mrs. Miller hurried away.

Sarah was awfully embarrassed. *I wonder if I should say I'm embarrassed by Mrs. Miller's matchmaking attempts*, she thought, *but then again, that would be criticizing Mrs. Miller. I wonder if there's something I could say.* Sarah could not think of anything to say, and so the two sat in silence for a moment. Finally, Sarah said, "Are you here alone?"

"*Jah*," Benjamin said, his cheeks flushing red. "Are you?"

"*Jah*, I mean *nee*, I'm here with Mrs. Miller."

"Oh of course, silly me."

The two laughed coyly. Sarah felt tongue-tied. Mrs. Miller chose that moment to reappear, and Sarah at first thought that was strange, given that Mrs. Miller was trying her hardest to be a matchmaker and had not left them alone for long.

"I've just popped back to let you know that I have to assist a friend. Can I meet you back here at noon, Sarah?"

"Sure, Mrs. Miller."

"I don't like to abandon you. Benjamin, would you do me a favor and escort Sarah around the mud sale until lunch time?"

"I'd be happy to, Mrs. Miller."

Mrs. Miller smiled at Benjamin and then hurried away, but Sarah was mortified. This time she felt she had to say something. "I'm so sorry, Benjamin. I don't want to be an imposition. I can find my own way around."

Benjamin beamed at her. "Nonsense! I will enjoy your company."

Sarah narrowed her eyes and stared into Benjamin's face. He did sound genuine. She hoped he was not just being polite.

"Sarah, where would you like to go first?" Benjamin smiled and held out his hand to Sarah.

Sarah took his hand, but he dropped hers as soon as she stood up, much to her disappointment. "I'm not sure, as I've never been to a mud sale before. Could we perhaps just walk around?"

"*Jah*, that's a *gut* idea."

An idea suddenly occurred to Sarah. "*Err*, you weren't here with anyone were you, or meeting someone?"

"*Nee*, I'm here alone. Or was," he added quietly.

Sarah's heart fluttered at his words, but she didn't know if he meant anything by them.

As Benjamin and Sarah walked side by side, she thought this would be what it would be like to be married, walking in happy companionship with her husband. There would be *bopplin* too, several of them.

Sarah was so lost in thought that she did not realize that Nash Grayson had suddenly materialized in front of them, right outside the horse auction tent. "What are you doing here?" she blurted out without thinking.

"I'm just looking for a horse for a friend. Not for a

horse as such, just seeing what prices the good ones go for. So I can tell my friend," he added.

Sarah frowned. Did Nash have any friends in the community? None that she knew of. Yet why would he lie?

"What are you doing here?" Nash directed the question at Benjamin.

"I'm on the volunteer firefighting crew."

Nash laughed, a dry, bitter laugh. "That figures."

"What do you mean?" Sarah did not mean to snap, but she was offended on Benjamin's behalf.

"Oh, I just mean that Benjamin is a good person. He's always doing good. It figures that he'd volunteer."

Sarah did not know what to make of Nash's words, but before she had time to formulate a response, a man led a tall black horse from the tent. The horse was prancing and side-stepping, and Sarah thought that the horse looked a little wild. The man nodded to Nash as if he knew him, and Nash looked uncomfortable. Just then the horse shied violently, and the man hurriedly led the horse away.

"Oh look!" Benjamin bent down and scooped up a tiny, scrawny kitten. "The poor little mite. This is what must have frightened the horse." Benjamin held the little kitten to his chest, and the kitten started to purr.

Sarah's heart melted. *He will make such a gut father*, she thought. *Look how compassionate and caring he is.* She reached over to stroke the little kitten, and Benjamin smiled at her. The two of them looked into each other's eyes for a moment, until Nash spoke.

"I saw some kids selling kittens, and it looks like

this is one of theirs. It must have got away from them."
He took the kitten from Benjamin, and cradled it,
looking into its little face and making cooing sounds
to it. "The kitten's half starved," he said angrily.
"Kitty, kitty, kitty, don't worry, you're safe now."

Benjamin and Sarah exchanged glances. Was this
the Nash Grayson they knew? "What are we going to
do with him?" Sarah asked Benjamin. "I'd take him,
only my cat Tom is set in his ways and might not take
kindly to a kitten, and besides, Mark Hostetler has
found a little kitten too. Mrs. Miller might not agree
to have yet another cat."

"I'd take him," Benjamin said, "but I wouldn't be
allowed to have a pet at the B&B."

"What's going on?"

The three turned around to see Jessie Yoder standing behind them, her hands on her hips. Without waiting for an answer, she took the kitten from Nash.
"Where did you find him?" she asked.

Benjamin was the one to answer. "He seems to be
a stray," he said, "or he might've escaped from some
children who were selling kittens. We were trying
to figure out what to do with him. I can't have him,
being at the B&B, and Sarah can't have him either."

"I could sneak him into my room," Nash said.

Jessie stroked the kitten. "Why, he needs a good
feed." She held the kitten close to her, and he purred
even more loudly than before. "My cat Calico died a
year ago. I had her since she was a kitten. I'm ready
to have another cat now. I'll take him."

"But I wanted him." Nash's voice sounded petulant.

"You can't have a cat at the B&B," Jessie said, but after a moment added, "We'll share him then. But he lives with me."

Nash smiled broadly, and he and Jessie walked away, their heads together, speaking in baby talk to the kitten.

Benjamin and Sarah stared after them in surprise.

Nash was a little annoyed that Benjamin Shetler was a volunteer on the firefighting crew. He'd never met such a do-gooder in all his life. Surely Benjamin had to be hiding something—no one could be *that* good, not even an Amish person. Besides, Nash was a little jealous and was concerned that Jessie might find Benjamin attractive. After all, Benjamin was a goody goody Amish man, whereas he was, well, a little on the wild side.

Nash sent up a silent prayer of thanks to *Gott* that Jessie had not seen him talking to the man about the horse. Nash did not have the money to buy a buggy horse, let alone a buggy yet, as he had to sell his car and pay his gambling debts first, but he wanted to make himself known to the horse dealers. And to think that he had nearly been caught looking at the horse by the self-righteous Benjamin Shetler. Oh well, there was no way that Benjamin would figure out he was talking to a dealer about his intention to buy a buggy horse later on, let alone returning to the community.

* * *

Jessie walked away with Nash, speaking to the kitten, which she was holding close to her. She was pleased she finally had found a replacement for her much loved cat, Calico. She was also pleased to see that Nash was so caring over the kitten. *He'll make a gut husband,* she thought. *He'll be gut to the kinner. I'll just have to straighten him out first.*

Chapter Twenty-Two

Sarah and Benjamin continued on their way, taking care not to step in the worst of the mud. "I suspect those two might be courting," Sarah said, expecting Benjamin to disagree.

"I think you might be right," he said with a chuckle. "I also think that Nash is in the market for a buggy horse."

"*Nee*! Really?" Sarah tugged on her prayer *kapp*. "That means that he's going to come back to the community."

Benjamin laughed. "*Jah*, and perhaps he wants to take a certain young lady on a buggy ride."

With that, the atmosphere at once turned from jovial and companionable to tense and drawn. Sarah was at once upset again that Benjamin had never asked her on a buggy ride, and after stealing a glance at Benjamin, she could see he was self-conscious too. Her happiness had fled, leaving a gloomy black cloud of disquiet in its place.

Still, the mud sale was not a place where one could remain miserable for long. "Goodness me," Sarah said, pointing to a strange creature standing beside a tall *Englischer*.

"That's an alpaca."

Sarah was intrigued. "What do they do?"

"They have fleece, like sheep, only they're far more expensive. Don't go too close," Benjamin warned. "Some of them spit, although that one looks friendly enough."

Sarah hung back, admiring the animal, and then stepped aside as two cute ponies were led past, their golden bodies contrasting with their long, white manes and tails.

"Oh they're so cute," Sarah gushed.

Benjamin chuckled. "A little too short for you to ride."

"They'd be *gut* for *kinner*." Sarah rolled her eyes at her own stupidity as soon as she said the words. *How could I be so thoughtless*, she thought, *saying that so soon after Benjamin mentioned the buggy ride?* She stole a glance at Benjamin and saw that he too was most uncomfortable, to the extent of wringing his hands.

"At least it's warm today," Benjamin said, interrupting the silence. "I went to a mud sale earlier in spring and I froze."

Sarah agreed, and they walked off again. The noise was overwhelming, and it seemed that every large tent had an auctioneer making a sound that to Sarah seemed like yodeling. In one tent there were Amish quilts of every type and size, and Sarah made a mental note to return there later with Mrs. Miller. Another tent was full of antiques, and the bidding was spirited. Yet another tent had all kinds of furniture, dressers, tables, and chairs, and the area outside the tents was just as crowded. One tent was filled with all types of well-groomed buggy horses, along with mules, and even adorable little ponies. Everywhere Sarah looked, she could see lumber, plants, field sprayers, pressure washers, lawn tractors, walk-behind mowers, manure spreaders, wood saws, rakes, as well as buggies.

"It's so kind of people to donate so many things," she said. "This mud sale should raise a lot of money."

Benjamin agreed. "It's needed, that's for sure. The fire trucks need updating, and the building is quite old. They want to replace it as soon as they can."

Just then a rowdy group of English teenagers ran past them, knocking Sarah over. They didn't stop, but disappeared into the crowd. Benjamin helped her to her feet and held onto her arms, his face full of concern. "Are you hurt?"

Sarah shook her head. "*Nee*, just shaken. What happened?"

"I'm not sure, it happened so fast. Are you sure you're okay? You're trembling."

Sarah was, in fact, trembling because of Benjamin's close proximity to her. He smelled comforting, and of leather, wood smoke, and handmade oatmeal soap. "Sorry."

"What for?" Benjamin finally released her arms.

"You're always helping me up."

Benjamin smiled warmly. "I'm not complaining."

Is he flirting with me? Sarah wondered. *I don't understand him. He acts if he likes me, but he never follows through.*

Benjamin took Sarah's arm, which sent tingles coursing through her and set off what felt like a thousand butterflies taking flight in her stomach. "You're still shaking. You had better sit down." He looked around and then pointed. "Over there."

A sign, 'Chicken corn soup take outs and chicken pot pie,' hung from a small, painted wooden building with a gray tiled roof. Visitors streamed in and out.

Sarah went to walk, but her ankle gave way under her, and she would have fallen again if not for Benjamin seizing her around her waist. His muscular arm around her waist set Sarah off into a fresh bout of trembling.

Benjamin appeared alarmed. "I'll fetch a *doktor*."

Sarah hurried to reassure him. "*Nee, nee*, Benjamin, I'm all right. I can walk, I think, slowly. I must've just twisted it when I fell." *I can hardly tell Benjamin that he's the one making me tremble*, she thought, *and no doktor can fix that*.

With Benjamin's hand on her arm, Sarah walked slowly to the building. They managed to find a little, vacant table pushed up against the far corner, with two seats, which they quickly claimed. "How is your foot now?" Benjamin asked.

"Better now that I'm sitting down. It will be all right, I'm sure." Sarah was grateful for Benjamin's concern. *He would make a wonderful husband*, she thought, and then silently chided herself for thinking such a thing.

Benjamin went away to see what food was on offer, and then soon returned. "There's chicken corn soup, chicken pot pie, pretzel log rolls, and you can have the pretzel stuffed with ham, roast beef, or sausage, with cheese. Oh, I forgot the rest. I'll be right back."

Sarah smiled at him. "*Nee*, that's fine. Would you get me a pretzel stuffed with sausage please and some hot tea with sugar, no cream?" Sarah opened her purse but Benjamin waved his hand at her.

"*Nee, nee*, allow me."

"*Denki*, Benjamin." *Oh why doesn't he like me?* she lamented, watching Benjamin's departing back.

Benjamin returned with the food, and the two enjoyed the easy conversation for a while. "How is your ankle now?" he asked when they had finished their meal.

Sarah stood up to test it. "A little sore, but it's taking my weight fine now."

Benjamin nodded. "*Gut*. Well, we must be getting you back to Mrs. Miller."

Sarah and Benjamin walked away, slowly, Sarah downcast that her time with Benjamin was drawing to a close.

Before they reached the fire hall, Benjamin stopped walking, so Sarah did the same. "I've enjoyed this time with you, today, Sarah."

Sarah smiled, encouraged by his words. "I have too, Benjamin," she said shyly.

He smiled tenderly and then continued walking.

That night, Sarah lay in bed, watching the rain fall through the window. She jumped as a lightning flash lighted up the night sky, and then jumped again when it was followed soon after by a deafening crack of thunder. *I hope the lightning doesn't strike anything*, she thought.

Sarah was glad the rain had not fallen earlier that day and ruined her time with Benjamin. Yet what good had that time done her? Benjamin had been attentive and sweet, but it seemed he did not want to court her. He had certainly made no move to do so and he had certainly had every opportunity.

Sarah had spent a restless night thinking about Benjamin. She had, in fact, spent many a restless night thinking about Benjamin, but this time it was different.

Benjamin had been acting as though he was attracted to her, and he had asked her if she was pleased that he was staying. Yet he had still not asked her on a buggy ride, even after their time alone together at the mud sale, not to mention the little café earlier.

Why? That was the question that had kept Sarah awake most of the night. Did Benjamin have another girl? If he was staying in the community, then it followed that any such girl would likely be in the community. And while it was common for courting couples to keep their courtships secret, Sarah was sure she would have heard whispers if indeed Benjamin was dating a girl from the community. This community was not too good with secrets, unlike her community.

Sarah had spent the morning helping at Hannah's *haus* and returned after lunch. She was unprepared for the shock that awaited her. There were three people sitting in the living room: Mr. Miller, Mrs. Miller, and her *vadder*, Samuel Beachy.

Sarah gasped in dismay. Her *vadder* was clearly there to fetch her back. What would she do?

The tension in the room was palpable. Mr. Miller had an unusually stern look on his face. Mrs. Miller was wringing her hands, and Samuel Beachy looked cross. He at once stood up. "Sarah, I've been so worried about you. Why didn't you let me know that you were all right?"

Sarah stood there, not knowing what to say. "*Err*, didn't Benjamin tell you?" she said lamely.

"*Nee*. At first he did say you were all right and staying with the Millers, but he refused to say any more, and I haven't had a letter from him in a very long time." Samuel Beachy shook his head in annoyance.

Sarah's heart leaped. So Benjamin hadn't been reporting back to her father after all! Despite the situation, a wave of happiness washed over her.

Samuel Beachy walked over to Sarah. "Sarah, child, I was so worried. I know we parted on bad terms, but it's time for you to come home now. The Millers have told me that you know everything now."

"I'll make us all a nice meadow tea," Mrs. Miller said, and hurried to the kitchen.

"I'll get some firewood," Mr. Miller said, and, although it was spring and the weather was warm, he hurried outside.

Sarah jutted out her chin in defiance. "I'm not coming home."

Samuel Beachy rubbed his *baard*. "I know you're angry with me, but your *mudder* made me promise not to tell you. We argued about it many a time."

"It's not that, *Datt*. My home is here now. I like living here."

Mr. Beachy sighed in exasperation. "You can't refuse to come home."

"I do refuse, *Datt*." Sarah's tone turned to pleading. "I'm not a child anymore, and I won't go back. My life is here now."

Mr. Beachy turned bright red and his eyes bulged. "We will speak about this later today. Think this over until then, and I trust you will come to your senses. I'm going to walk to the B&B now, and I'll be staying there. I also want to speak with Benjamin about how he let me down."

"He let you down?" Sarah knew she shouldn't continue the conversation when her *daed* was in this mood, but curiosity got the better of her.

"*Jah*," he snapped. "I sent Benjamin to encourage you to return and to bring you back. I didn't come to fetch you because I knew you would only run away again. The bishop of this community knows all this. When I sent Benjamin here, I gave him a letter to take to the bishop."

Sarah shouldn't have been surprised, as what her

daed said was only to be expected, but she sat down and fought back the tears. She had made a nice home for herself here with the Millers, and was *gut* friends with Mary and the Miller *schweschders*. This was the first happy *familye* life she had ever known. Her upbringing had been lonely, with being the only child, and her *mudder* had been stern and undemonstrative.

Sarah looked around the living room in the *haus* she had grown to love. There was a wood fire against one wall, a wall that was white like the others throughout the *haus*. The only colors to be seen were brown and blue, the brown being the heavy wooden furniture. The old, comfortable armchairs were blue, and had various quilts and crocheted blankets thrown over them. Yet while to an outsider, the room might look plain and sparse, to Sarah it was filled with the love of *familye*.

Mrs. Miller returned with mugs of tea. "*Denki*, Rachel," Samuel said, "but I had best be going to the B&B to settle in, and have a word with Benjamin Shetler."

"I hope you will return soon," Mrs. Miller said.

"*Jah*, I would like to return in a few hours to speak with Sarah again, if that would be all right."

Mrs. Miller nodded. "That would be *gut*."

As soon as Samuel left, Sarah walked over to sit at the kitchen table and Mrs. Miller joined her. "He's gone to the B&B to speak to Benjamin." Sarah was doing her best not to cry.

"Do not worry, it's all *gut*," Mrs. Miller said.

"But *Datt* wants me to go home with him."

"Sarah, you're a grown woman now. Your *vadder* can't make you go home with him; he can simply try to pressure you to. The decision is entirely yours."

"I'd like to stay here with you, that is, if you'll allow me too?"

Mrs. Miller looked pleased. "Of course you may stay with us, as long as you like."

Sarah was relieved. It was as if a huge weight had been lifted off her shoulders. As soon as her *daed* had shown up, Sarah had been harboring the fear that Mrs. Miller would ask her to leave. Sarah had worried that Mrs. Miller might think it was the right thing to do, for her to be with her *vadder*.

Chapter Twenty-Three

Benjamin had been outside, enjoying the spring air, when Jessie Yoder approached him. "I need to speak with you in private," she said.

Benjamin was perplexed. "What is it?"

Jessie motioned him to move to the side of the building, behind a cluster of trees. "I think you should know about a new booking." Her voice was low and hushed.

Benjamin was even more puzzled, but waited for Jessie to continue.

"Samuel Beachy has booked here for the week, and he arranged a cab to collect him from the bus station this morning," she whispered.

Benjamin gasped. "Is he here yet?"

Jessie shrugged. "Not as far as I know. I figure he'd have gone straight to the Millers."

Benjamin thought for a moment. "So you know all about Sarah?"

"*Jah*." Jessie nodded. "I know she's a Miller and

all that, and that you were sent here to fetch her back home. Fannie Graber, the bishop's wife, told my *mudder* and told her she mustn't tell anyone. My *mudder* told me and told me I mustn't tell anyone. Nash told me too, but I already knew. Don't tell Nash though, I don't want him to know that I already knew ages before he told me."

"Oh." Benjamin was still perplexed, even more so at Jessie's matter-of-fact tone and then again by the fact that she was trying to trick Nash, when the two of them always seemed to be as thick as thieves. "Well, *denki* for telling me. It was *gut* of you."

Jessie narrowed her eyes at him. "Do you want some advice?"

Benjamin would have liked to say, *No, not really*, but instead said, "Okay." He was far too polite to speak his mind, especially to such a puzzling and forbidding person as Jessie Yoder.

"Have you asked Sarah on a buggy ride yet?"

"*Nee.*" Benjamin didn't see it was any of Jessie's business, and what's more, it was a question rather than the promised advice, but he did not know how to avoid answering her question.

"Why not?"

"Err, um, err, um." The situation was growing even more uncomfortable. Benjamin had never been so embarrassed in his whole, entire life. What on earth could he say?

Jessie persisted. "You want to, don't you?"

"*Jah*, of course." At least that was one question he had no hesitation in answering.

"I said I'd give you my advice, and this is it, so you can take it or leave it. I don't know what your problem is, but you should've asked her on a buggy ride ages ago. It's obvious she really likes you—any fool can see that. So my advice is to ask her on a buggy ride next time you see her, especially with her *vadder* here to take her back." With that, Jessie looked him up and down, and then left.

Benjamin stood there, watching her walk away. He felt like some sort of insect that had been examined and then nearly squashed.

Nash Grayson was peeking through the curtains at Jessie, and saw her walk over to Benjamin. He hurried down the stairs, but the two had vanished. He crept around the side of the building until he saw them under the trees, their heads close together. Whatever was going on? Was this some kind of tryst? Surely they hadn't been courting without him knowing.

Nash crept around some more but was unable to get closer. When Jessie turned to leave, he hurried back to his room to think things over. He was determined to get to the bottom of this. Nash peeked through his window again and this time saw an Amish man walking up the road carrying a suitcase. There was no one else in sight. Benjamin had disappeared too.

Nash sneaked down the stairs to hear who the Amish man was. Jessie was checking him in due to the fact that Nash's parents, the Flickingers, were away for the afternoon, visiting. The man gave his name, and Nash lost interest. He was about to return to his room when he heard the man ask to speak to Benjamin Shetler.

Nash's ears pricked up. Perhaps Benjamin had gambling debts too, and this man was here to collect. Benjamin was just too nice to be on the level. Nash was sure he was up to something. If Nash could get some dirt on Benjamin, then he would present it to Jessie, and she would see the type of man Benjamin truly was.

Nash crouched behind the corner as Jessie left, presumably in search of Benjamin. Nash peeked around the wall to see the man sinking into the upholstery of a comfortable, oak sleigh sofa. *Make yourself at home, why don't you*, Nash thought.

It seemed like forever before Benjamin entered the B&B, but it was probably only five or so minutes. There was no sign of Jessie. Nash assumed she had gone to clean or to do laundry. At any rate, the man had said he wanted to speak to Benjamin, so Jessie would of course make herself scarce.

Nash had taken up a good position around the corner. He was not willing to peep, as Benjamin would likely be facing him, so he set himself to overhear the conversation. He fervently hoped Benjamin was in some kind of trouble, and he was already looking forward to telling Jessie all about it.

To Nash's disappointment, the two men appeared to greet each other amicably enough, although Nash managed to overhear the older man telling Benjamin that he should have reported back to him. What Nash heard was interesting, but provided him with no ammunition against Benjamin, much to his frustration.

Nash was dissatisfied. *Is that all there is to it?* he thought. *The man just wanted Benjamin to report to him, no big deal. I was hoping Benjamin was some sort of criminal, so Jessie would turn her back on him.*

Nevertheless, Nash strained his ears to hear more, and was delighted with what he heard. *Jessie won't want Benjamin after this*, he gloated to himself.

"What are you doing?"

Nash spun around to see Jessie regarding him sternly, her hands on her hips.

He held his finger to his lips. "*Shush!* What does it look like I'm doing?"

"Listening in to someone else's conversation."

Nash smirked at her. "That's right. Well since you already knew, why did you ask?"

Jessie sighed. She took Nash by the arm and led him outside. "Haven't you heard the old saying, *'Eavesdroppers never hear any good of themselves'*?"

Nash snorted rudely. "Ouch, that hurt. Anyway, they weren't talking about me. The man turns out to be Sarah's father, and Benjamin was telling him that he's going to ask Sarah to marry him." Nash carefully watched Jessie's face for any sign of shock or disappointment.

"*Wunderbar!*" she exclaimed.

Nash was taken aback. "You're happy?"

"Of course, why wouldn't I be?" Jessie scowled at Nash.

"I thought you liked Benjamin," he blurted out. "I saw the two of you talking earlier."

Jessie smirked at him. "We were talking about Sarah, not that it's any of your concern."

"Sarah?" Nash took a moment to process the information. "So you don't like Benjamin?"

Jessie shook her head in frustration. "Of course I don't like Benjamin Shetler. He's not my type. I like…"

"Who?" Nash prompted. "Who? Who do you like?" When Jessie didn't answer, he continued. "You like me, don't you?" He held his breath, anxiously awaiting her answer.

"*Jah.*" Jessie stuck out her bottom lip. "I don't know why."

Nash was overjoyed, but tried not to show it. "Then will you go on that buggy ride with me?" He kept his tone even, and tried to look as though he didn't care about the answer.

Jessie raised one eyebrow. "You don't have a buggy." Before Nash could continue, she added, "*Jah,* I will go on a buggy ride with you, but only if you agree to come back to the community and get baptized."

Nash scratched his head and pretended to think it over. "You drive a hard bargain," he said after a few moments. "But I will agree on one condition, that you give up smoking."

Jessie rubbed her chin and covered her mouth with her hand. Finally, she looked up at him. "You drive a hard bargain too. Okay, I agree to give up smoking. I suppose that's only fair."

Nash could barely contain his excitement. He knew that Jessie was the woman of his dreams. He considered himself blessed by *Gott*, and also blessed in that, as clever as Jessie was, he was able to outsmart her. He congratulated himself on tricking her into giving up smoking. Not only that, he had already decided to go back to the community and be baptized. Why, he'd even spoken to the bishop about it earlier that week. Best to let Jessie think he was doing it because she asked him to, he figured. He knew how to handle women.

Jessie walked away, elated, and she sent up a silent prayer of thanks to *Gott*. *I know how to handle menner*, she thought. *Nash is a pushover. He didn't even know I'd already given up smoking, but best to let him think I gave up because he asked me to.*

Jessie was beside herself with happiness. Clearly Nash was the *mann* of her dreams; she had known that from the first moment she had laid eyes on him. Only he wasn't as clever as he thought he was. He had easily given in when she asked him to go back to the Amish and be baptized. Jessie chuckled aloud, pleased with the thought that she would be able to outsmart her future husband.

Chapter Twenty-Four

Sarah was at a loss. Whatever was she to do? Sure, her *vadder* had gone for the moment, but he was likely to come back at any time. She could not go home with him; she just couldn't. Yet would he make a scene when she refused to go? Sarah did not like unpleasantness. She paced up and down until a frustrated Mrs. Miller told her to keep herself busy by preparing food.

It was only a few hours before Samuel Beachy returned to the Miller *haus*, but even so, Sarah had already made a pile of *Faasnachtkuche*, potato-based donuts, as well as several whoopie pies and an apple cake. She had just taken a baking dish of John Cope's Corn, nicely browned, from the oven. The backs of two kitchen chairs were covered with rolled dough hanging in strips to dry before cutting for a large pot pie.

Sarah wrung her hands anxiously when Mrs. Miller let Sarah's *vadder*, Samuel Beachy, into the *haus* and showed him to the living room and insisted he sit down. "I'll fetch Abraham," Mrs. Miller said.

Samuel Beachy held up his hand. "*Nee*, that won't be necessary. Sarah, I've just come to say that, after a long talk with Benjamin, I've decided that I will not insist that you come home."

Sarah could scarcely believe her ears. What did Benjamin have to do with it? Whatever did he say to convince her *vadder* to let her stay?

"But I hope you'll come visit me often," her *vadder* continued, and then turned to Mrs. Miller. "And if I may, Rachel, I'd like to stay at the Flickingers' B&B for a week and visit with Sarah while I'm here."

Mrs. Miller was clearly delighted. "That would be *wunderbar*, Samuel. *Denki* for this. Yes, you are *wilkom* to visit us, not just this week, but Abraham and I would like you to visit us often in the future. Also, please visit with us for dinner tonight."

"*Denki*." Samuel smiled.

Sarah had rarely seen her *vadder* smile, and she realized only now that he must have been carrying a burden for many years, the burden of keeping, at his *fraa's* instance, the secret of Sarah's true *vadder*. She realized at that moment that it was not wise to judge people's actions without a full understanding of their circumstances.

Samuel stood up from the chair where he had been so briefly sitting. "Sarah, can we go for a walk so we can talk?"

Sarah looked nervously at Mrs. Miller, who smiled encouragingly. "Sure, *Datt*," she said.

The two walked outside the Miller *haus*. Samuel stopped at the gate. "Sarah, you're at the age where you will be getting married soon, so I want to reconnect with you and repair our relationship."

Sarah had no idea what to say, so simply said, "*Jah, Datt*, that would be *gut*."

They walked down the lane, at first in silence, but then Samuel spoke. "Sarah, I'm sorry I deceived you all these years."

Sarah hurried to reassure him. "I know you had no choice. It was *Mamm's* wishes."

Samuel nodded, and after they had wandered down the winding lane for a while, he indicated they should sit on a fallen tree branch, which was nestled amongst a tangle of rhododendron and laurel thickets. It was a Box Elder maple, and the fallen branch, which had obviously fallen some time ago, was still sprouting leaves and green branches. Sarah sat on the smooth bark and looked at the young branches. It was then that she had a thought. She was like a young, green shoot, and her *daed* was the branch, strong and stout. He may not have been her biological *vadder*, but he was her *vadder* just the same, equally so.

"Sarah," her father began, in a faltering voice, "I had two reasons for not telling you the truth after your *mudder* died."

Sarah turned to look at him expectantly.

"The first reason was that I was afraid of your reaction when you found out that I'd been deceiving you all these years, and the second reason was that I was afraid you wouldn't love me anymore when you found out that I was not your real *vadder*."

"You *are* my real *vadder*," Sarah said quietly.

"*Denki*." Samuel looked at Sarah and smiled.

Sarah smiled too. She wanted to hug him, but her parents had never been demonstrative with their feelings.

"Do you hear that?"

Sarah put her head to one side. "It sounds like someone playing a flute. What is it?"

"It's the male wood thrush," Samuel said. "He makes the most beautiful sound of all birds."

Sarah had to agree. "It is such a melodic sound. But *Datt*, I didn't know that you knew anything about birds?"

Samuel chuckled, and a rare grin spread across his face. "Birding was my hobby as a child and a young man, but your *mudder* said it was a waste of time. Oh, forgive me. I don't mean to criticize your *mudder*."

"Oh no, I understand." Sarah watched as a pretty, cinnamon brown bird with brown spotting against a cream background on its chest flew into the tree above her. A large worm dangled from its mouth.

"That must be the mother wood thrush," Samuel explained. "The females do not sing."

Sarah thought how parents care for the *kinner*; even the parent birds looked after their young. She thought of the Scripture from the Gospel of Matthew that the ministers often read: *Behold the fowls of the air: for they sow not, neither do they reap, nor gather*

into barns; yet your heavenly Father feedeth them.
Are ye not much better than they?

Sarah truly understood that Scripture for the first time.

A small stream meandered beside the road, and five obedient ducklings were following their mother along the bank. Sarah looked out over the gently rolling hills, over the lush, green fields with contented cows grazing on them, to the white-painted, red-roofed barns in the distance.

Sitting there with her *daed* was a treasure. Being with *familye* was one of the simple pleasures of life, and one of the most important.

Chapter Twenty-Five

Sarah had enjoyed the week, with her *vadder* visiting for dinner with the Millers every night. The day before he was to leave, Sarah returned from taking sewing to Mrs. Hostetler in the late afternoon to see her *vadder* and Mrs. Miller sitting at the kitchen table, talking.

Samuel smiled at Sarah. "Sarah, Benjamin's waiting for you down by the pond."

"He is?" Sarah was puzzled, and saw both her *vadder* and Mrs. Miller exchange a smile.

"Off you go then, Sarah. Don't just stand here with your mouth open." With that, Mrs. Miller shooed Sarah out of the *haus*.

Sarah made her way down to the pond, wondering why Benjamin was waiting for her. Her mind felt clouded, but the day was beautiful, and she walked slowly, enjoying the scent carried along on the gentle breeze of the blue-topped rosemary and lavender bushes in the herb garden, and by the deep red, old

English roses that bordered the fence. She looked up at the glorious blue and brown colors of the purple martins chirping happily from their martin houses. Spring was filled with bright colors and charming sounds, and filled with the promise of endless possibilities.

Sarah was a little nervous as to why Benjamin was waiting for her, but she figured it must be a *gut* thing. If he had been dating someone else, he would surely have told her already. After all, he'd had plenty of chances to do so at the café and the mud sale. Little tingles of excitement ran through her as she made her way down the winding, dirt road that ran by the pond.

As Sarah approached the pond, she saw Benjamin standing there. He was everything she loved. He was kind; he was good; he was a *mann* of *Gott*. Sarah walked up to stand in front of him.

Benjamin's strong jaw softened when he saw Sarah. He walked straight to her and stopped, towering over her. "Have you been baking?"

Sarah nodded. She had not expected to hear those words. "How did you know?"

Benjamin laughed, and with one finger, wiped flour off the tip of her nose. "Flour," he said, smiling.

Sarah smiled too. She felt the presence of *Gott* in this calm, tranquil place, with the *mann* she loved standing in front of her. All seemed at once right with the world.

"Sarah you look beautiful. You *are* beautiful, inside and out. You are a vision of loveliness." He took both Sarah's hands in his.

Sarah wished the sun was not so bright, as she blushed horribly, and given the fact her cheeks were burning, was sure her face had flushed beet red. She simply looked up at Benjamin and did not speak. Who knows how long the two would have stood there, had they not been broken apart by a duck suddenly taking flight from the pond.

Benjamin took both Sarah's hands in his. "Sarah Beachy, would you honor me by agreeing to become my *fraa*?"

Sarah gasped and then stood there with her mouth open. She had certainly not expected this. The most she had hoped for was a buggy ride, which he still had not mentioned. She looked at Benjamin and saw disappointment and concern on his face, so she hastened to say, "*Jah*, of course I'll marry you, Benjamin."

Benjamin's face lighted up like a chorus of angels. "Oh thank goodness," he said with relief.

Sarah too was relieved, as well as beside herself with delight. This was all she had ever wanted, but she was still puzzled. One question remained unanswered. "Benjamin, why haven't you ever asked me on a buggy ride?"

Benjamin flushed red. "I'm very shy, Sarah."

"Shy?" Sarah looked up into Benjamin's big, brown eyes. "But I always thought you were confident."

Benjamin shook his head. "*Nee*, not when it came to you. I've loved you for as long as I can remember, but I was far too shy to ask you on a buggy ride.

I was afraid you'd say *No* and I wouldn't have been able to bear that."

Sarah frowned. Silly as it seemed, she wanted that buggy ride. "We can go on a buggy ride though, can't we?"

Benjamin laughed. It was the loveliest sound Sarah had ever heard. "Of course. We'll go on a buggy ride tomorrow, and we will go on as many buggy rides as you'd ever like, for many years to come."

Benjamin drew Sarah to him. "Sarah," he whispered.

"Yes, Benjamin?"

"There's not a man in this world who is happier than I am at this moment. *Gott* has truly blessed us." Benjamin looked adoringly into Sarah's eyes.

Sarah could feel her heart race as she looked into her beloved's brown eyes. Her eyes dropped to his lips and she hoped he would soon kiss her so she could taste his lips. At that moment Benjamin, as if reading her mind, lowered his warm lips to hers and with his arm around her waist, pulled her close to him.

As their lips met tenderly, Sarah silently thanked *Gott* for blessing her so abundantly.

Some years later on a summer evening, Mrs. Miller sat looking at her married *dochders*, Hannah, Esther, Martha, Rebecca, and Sarah—for she considered Sarah a *dochder*—with their husbands and their *kinner*: Hannah's twins, and another two girls, Esther's three boys, Martha's two girls and one boy,

Rebecca's three girls, and Sarah's two boys. Mary and David had one boy and one girl.

Gott had truly blessed the Millers with a large *familye*.

Mrs. Miller smiled across the room at her *gut* friend, Betsy Yoder, whose *dochder*, Jessie, was despairing over her two cute yet mischievous little boys. They had snatched the little wooden toys from Sarah's two boys and were trying to hit them over the head with them. Their *vadder*, Nash, who had long since gone back to his birth name of Eli, was trying to discipline them. "I don't know why they're always so naughty," he complained.

Mrs. Miller thought back on the previous years, from the time of the buggy accident until now, and was amazed how *Gott* had turned all their sorrow into laughter. "No matter how it looks at the time, all things work together for good for those who love *Gott*," she said aloud, and everyone said, *"Amen."*

* * * * *

SPECIAL EXCERPT FROM

🌿

LOVE INSPIRED
INSPIRATIONAL ROMANCE

*When a city slicker wants the same piece of land
as a small-town girl, will sparks fly between them?*

Read on for a sneak preview of
Opening Her Heart
by Deb Kastner.

What on earth?

Suddenly, a shiny red Mustang came around the curve
of the driveway at a speed far too fast for the dirt road,
and when the vehicle slammed to a stop, it nearly hit the
side of Avery's SUV.

Who drove that way, especially on unpaved mountain
roads?

The man unfolded himself from the driver's seat and
stood to his full over-six-foot height, let out a whoop of
pure pleasure and waved his black cowboy hat in the air
before combing his fingers through his thick dark hair
and settling the hat on his head.

Avery had never seen him before in her life.

It wasn't so much that they didn't have strangers
occasionally visiting Whispering Pines. Avery's own
family brought in customers from all over Colorado who
wanted the full Christmas tree–cutting experience.

So, yes, there were often strangers in town.

But this man?

He was as out of place as a blue spruce in an orange grove. And he was on land she intended to purchase—before anyone else was supposed to know about it.

Yes, he sported a cowboy hat and boots similar to those that the men around the Pines wore, but his whole getup probably cost more than Avery made in a year, and his new boots gleamed from a fresh polish.

Avery fought to withhold a grin, thinking about how quickly those shiny boots would lose their luster with all the dirt he'd raised with his foolish driving.

Served him right.

Just what was this stranger doing *here*?

"And didn't you say the cabin wasn't listed yet?" Avery said quietly. "What does this guy think he's doing here?"

"I have no idea how—" Lisa whispered back.

"Good afternoon, ladies," said the man as he tipped his hat, accompanied by a sparkle in his deep blue eyes and a grin Avery could only categorize as charismatic. He could easily have starred in a toothpaste commercial.

She had a bad feeling about this.

As the man approached, the puppy at Avery's heels started barking and straining against his lead—something he'd been in training not to do. Was he trying to protect her, to tell her this man was bad news?

Don't miss
Opening Her Heart *by Deb Kastner,*
available January 2021 wherever
Love Inspired books and ebooks are sold.

LoveInspired.com

LIEXP1220

IF YOU ENJOYED THIS BOOK
WE THINK YOU WILL ALSO LOVE

⟨H⟩ HARLEQUIN
SPECIAL
EDITION

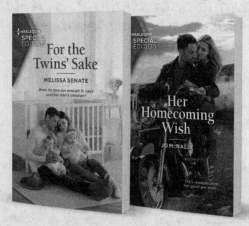

Believe in love. Overcome obstacles. Find happiness.

Relate to finding comfort and strength in the
support of loved ones and enjoy the journey
no matter what life throws your way.

6 NEW BOOKS AVAILABLE EVERY MONTH!

Love Harlequin romance?

DISCOVER.

Be the first to find out about promotions,
news and exclusive content!

 Facebook.com/HarlequinBooks

Twitter.com/HarlequinBooks

 Instagram.com/HarlequinBooks

Pinterest.com/HarlequinBooks

ReaderService.com

EXPLORE.

Sign up for the Harlequin e-newsletter and
download a free book from any series at
TryHarlequin.com

CONNECT.

Join our Harlequin community to
share your thoughts and connect
with other romance readers!
Facebook.com/groups/HarlequinConnection

HSOCIAL2020